Honeymoon for Five

CHRIS KENISTON

Indie House Publishing

MORE BOOKS
By Chris Keniston

Hart Land
Heather
Lily
Violet
Iris
Hyacinth
Rose
Calytrix
Zinnia
Poppy
Picture Perfect

Farraday Country
Adam
Brooks
Connor
Declan
Ethan
Finn
Grace
Hannah
Ian
Jamison
Keeping Eileen
Loving Chloe
Morgan
Neil
Owen

Honeymoon Series
Honeymoon for One
Honeymoon for Three
Honeymoon for Four
Honeymoon for Five
Honeymoon for Six

Aloha Romance Series:
Aloha Texas
Almost Paradise
Mai Tai Marriage
Dive Into You
Look of Love
Love by Design
Love Walks In
Shell Game
Flirting with Paradise

Surf's Up Flirts:
(Aloha Series Companions)
Shall We Dance
Love on Tap
Head Over Heels
Perfect Match
Just One Kiss
It Had to Be You
Cat's Meow

ACKNOWLEDGMENTS

Hello again!

I hope you've all had a wonderful time since my last release. I have been working hard to get new series started while finishing up Honeymoon for Five. This idea came to me over dinner with my dear friend Roberta Eichenberger. Thank you.

I've been blessed with friends who let me call them in a panic at all hours of the night as I get stuck on the dreaded...*now what*? Thank you for being there and being patient as always authors Kathy Ivan and Susan Warner. For encouraging me no matter how busy she is, thank you Dale Mayer. Nothing beats good friends, except maybe family. One more contribution that needs to be mentioned. I have been blessed with a supportive ARC team and one in particular Christina Stevens gets all the credit for the scene in the cove!

Now, on to the first of three sisters finding love on the high seas! Thanks for joining me for the ride!

CHAPTER ONE

"**I** absolutely love the smell of spring." Mina Ummarino stood on her next door neighbor's back porch and sniffed at the air like a dog taking in the scent of a sizzling steak.

"Smell?" Jo, her younger and more technical sister, scrunched her face and shook her head. "The only thing we can smell out here is the exhaust from MacArthur Avenue."

"Aren't we in a mood?" Melody Harwood teased the sisters. "You guys can argue about whether the air smells of rain or flowers or cat litter for all I care. Five more days and Shane and I will be basking under glorious Caribbean skies."

"Oh." Jo spun around and flopped into the rocker. "Ever since my sisters and I bought the house next door to Angie and heard all the great stories, I've added a cruise to my bucket list. They sound like so much fun. I just hope that I don't have to wait till my honeymoon to take one."

Mina nodded. She hoped the same thing. No matter her intentions of getting some friends together and having a seaside vacation like her friend and neighbor Angie, life had a way of always making other plans. Days flew by too fast. Chores and responsibilities, and of course family always came first. Spontaneity was a foreign word to her. She really would have to make more of an effort if she wanted to pull off a friends' vacation.

"The only thing that would have made this little honeymoon trip of ours even better would have been if we had been able to take it right after the wedding instead of a year later, but it's still going to be so sweet." Melody handed a diet cola to Mina and chuckled. "At least I'm all packed and ready to go."

"About that." Shane Harwood, a tall man dressed in military camo, came out the kitchen door.

Melody turned and flashed a sappy grin at her spouse that made all the sisters on the porch smile. Love really was fun to watch.

The moment Melody's eyes leveled with her husband's, the sweet grin slipped. "What's wrong?"

"Orders."

"One word and already I don't like the sound of that."

Shane blew out a sigh and pulled his wife into the curve of his shoulder. "All leaves are cancelled. We're shipping out ASAP. I've got to collect my bag and report to base."

"But…" Her head tipped back and she stared into steely gray eyes. "The trip."

He bobbed his head. "I can't do anything about it. Unless all the nutcase leaders in the world suddenly grow common sense, things like this happen."

Lips pressed tightly together, Melody barely nodded. Anyone on the porch could see her fighting tears. "I know. There will be another time."

"We can't get any of our money back at this late hour. You should find a friend and go anyway."

Melody sprang out of his hold. "I don't want to go on the trip without you."

"I know." He curled her back into him. "But at least one of us should have a good time."

"I can't." Her head buried in his shoulder, she shook it left then right. "There is no way on earth that I'd take our dream trip without you."

His fingers drew casual circles on her back, and he leaned in to kiss the top of her head. "I know, honey. I'm really sorry. We will go another time. I promise."

Lowering his head, his lips met hers for a tender peck that turned a tad more heated for Mina's comfort, and she and her sisters developed a sudden interest in Melody's flower beds.

"I love you." He inched away, kissed her forehead, and took another long step in retreat.

"Love you more." Melody's hands fell to her side, her eyes still glistening with held back tears.

"My bag's in the front hall. I'll contact you as soon as I can."

Melody nodded and the four of them watched him walk down the hall, grab his bag and proceed out the front door. "And that's that."

Now Mina understood the old cliché about looking like someone just kicked your puppy. Melody had gone from cloud nine to the basement in a split second. "I think this calls for an Ummarino family dinner."

"Oh, for the love of St. Anthony," Ginnie shook her head, "she needs our family like she needs a hole in her head."

"Not the actual family." Honestly, Mina wondered how her sister could be so literal. "Just the meal. Nothing soothes the soul like fresh mozzarella melting in a homemade lasagna with toasted garlic bread and some of Mama's cannolis."

"She has a point." Jo smiled. "I think I have some of Mom's pizzelles in the freezer too."

"Then it's a plan." Mina pushed to her feet. "I'll hit Mom's kitchen and steal some of her sauce. We can have a nice family dinner and just in case, I'll pick up some butter pecan ice cream on my way home."

"No need." Ginnie shook her head again. "There's a gallon of butter pecan in the garage freezer."

Jo frowned at her sister. "You've been holding out on us. Where in the freezer?"

Grinning like a cat with a belly full of cream, Ginnie shrugged at the baby of the family. "It's behind the frozen spinach."

"I don't know." Melody leaned over the porch railing. "I may just curl up with a sappy book and stay in bed until Shane comes home."

"Nonsense." Mina sidled up by her neighbor. "I'll call Angie. We'll have a nice long girls' night, and for a little extra insurance, I'll bring over Dad's chianti."

Two hours and one bottle of wine later, the five women

were smiling, giggling, and diving into a fresh baked lasagna.

"You know," Angie stabbed at her dinner, "your husband had a good idea. When my friend who used to own Mina's house had her fiancé walk out on her, she took the trip alone. She had a great time."

Ginnie chuckled. "From your stories, everyone has a great time on a cruise."

"I know I did." Angie smiled.

"Wasn't that honeymoon cruise where your friend met her husband?" Jo asked.

Angie nodded. "It was."

"I don't need a husband." Melody pulled apart a piece of warm garlic bread and mid-bite, her eyes rounded, she held up a finger and quickly swallowed. "But two of you should go."

"Two of who?" Ginnie reached for her wine.

"You." Melody waved at the women around the table. "Draw straws or something."

"Not me." Angie shook her head. "Devon and I have plans and they don't include getting a week's vacation at the last minute."

"What about you three?" Melody looked almost as excited as she'd been before her husband dropped the unpleasant news.

Mina's knee-jerk reaction was *no way*. After all, there was work and chores and all those pesky little responsibilities, of which missing Sunday supper at her mother's was top of the list, that she had to consider. *Didn't she*? She actually had to stop and make herself think about it for a minute. She hadn't taken a vacation in so long that she had enough days off accumulated to take several cruises. And how horrible would it be to add a little spontaneity to her vocabulary? She tipped her head at her two sisters. "Maybe?"

"Really?" Ginnie snapped her mouth shut as soon as the word crossed her lips. "I was just thinking that, but I didn't think you'd be willing to, you know, just up and go."

"Perhaps it's time I planned a little less and just up and

did a little more." The whole situation made her wonder what else has she been missing out on by always postponing the unplanned.

A slow smile pulling at the corners of Ginnie's mouth. "Could be fun."

"Wait." Jo held up her hand. "Why do you two get to have all the fun? I have lots of vacation days I haven't used yet."

"Because we're older." Mina flashed her kid sister—who hadn't been a kid for a very long time—a toothy grin. They'd been pulling rank on her since the day she was born. Mina didn't know why her stomach wasn't revolting on her. She never did spur of the moment things like this, especially big things like this, but the whole idea was actually taking root and sprouting flowers. Fun colorful and exciting flowers.

"This age before beauty thing is getting worn out." Jo grinned widely, obviously proud of herself for the little twist on an age old dance the three sisters did.

"Before you guys start drawing straws," Angie waved her hands at them, "a lot of those cabins are equipped with extra bedding for families. Maybe you could call and add a person to the cabin."

"Do we know if we can even switch out names at this late hour?" In her mind, Mina was packing her bags and dreaming of lounging on a warm beach. It would be a shame if this couldn't work out.

"No problem," Angie spoke up. "Been there, done that. Cruise lines only need twenty-four hours to substitute passengers."

Mina looked at Ginnie then Jo, silently asking if they were going on a vacation. After all, they're Italian, deeply rooted in Latin, shouldn't *Carpe Diem*, seize the day, be ingrained in them somehow? The two sisters stole a sideways glance at each other, smiled and then turning back to Mina, nodded. "I guess we're going on a cruise!"

"Hey bro, I was just getting ready to call you. You'd be proud of me." Kent Harwood had just come from doing battle with his bosses' efforts to pull him into the latest upset. He'd given them plenty of notice for taking time off to dog sit for his brother's pack while Shane and his wife were off on their long-awaited cruise, someone else could step in and set the project right. He was actually looking forward to a little down time in a house with a yard, no stomping neighbors upstairs, no stereo playing teenagers next door, and not dealing with anything unpredictable for five whole business days. "I stuck to my guns at work and will be driving down day after tomorrow to play Uncle Kent to the pups."

"Yeah, about that."

Oh, he didn't like the sound of that. Through the years he'd learned to read his brother by the look in his eyes or tone of his voice. This tone was definitely shouting bad news coming. "What's wrong?"

"We're going wheels up. I can't take Melody on the cruise."

"Oh, man." The two had been looking forward to that cruise for so long he felt terrible for them. "How soon?"

"Very."

Another thing he'd learned about his brother's military career is that almost everything was on a need to know basis, and the family rarely ever needed to know. "Now what?"

"I'm already heading to base."

"Does Melody know?"

"Dude. She's my wife. Of course I told her first. And in person."

"Sorry." Even after almost a year, he still tended to forget his brother was now half of a whole. They'd been bachelors for so long and then Shane had met Melody. The two had meshed so hard and strong that within a few months they were engaged, and six months later they were standing in front of a preacher. They'd had to settle for a long weekend honeymoon in a local resort, but had this upcoming anniversary trip to look forward to. This was a crappy turn of events. "How can I help?" Not that he really expected to be much use, but if his brother, or sister-in-law, needed him for anything, he'd be there.

"How do you feel about taking a cruise?"

"Say again." Surely he hadn't heard that correctly. He didn't mind stepping in to help, but taking his sister-in-law on a cruise was not on his radar.

"I told Melody to take a girlfriend and go, but she doesn't want to without me."

"Can't say that I blame her."

"The cabin is paid for. Someone should use it, you've already got a week's vacation lined up and we don't need a dog sitter anymore."

"I don't know." He did have a week off, and spending that time on the blue Caribbean would certainly be the ultimate break, but… "Can I just take over your cabin? I mean, this isn't like a dinner reservation."

"Yeah, it's surprisingly easy. I checked before talking to Melody to make sure a friend could take my place."

Which meant, unless he wanted to reimburse his brother for the whole thing, he needed to find a travel buddy and probably fast. "How long do I have to think about this?"

"You've got two days. After that, the twenty four-hour deadline will kick in and no one except Melody and me would be able to travel, and on such short notice, there's no time to put this out there."

His brother was right. Time was of the essence, and as long as there was wifi on the ship, he should be able to talk a buddy into joining him. "Okay. I'll do it."

"Great. That will take a load off of us. I'll forward you all the reservation info shortly. I'm almost at the base."

Now Kent wanted to say something dorky like stay safe, or keep your head down, but after all these years, he'd learned to keep his concerns to himself. "I'll take care of it. I'll also make sure your wife knows to count on me if she needs anything while you're away."

"Thanks, man. I hate leaving her like this, but it is what it is. Hopefully none of this will last long and I'll be home sooner than later."

"Amen." He thought that every time his brother was deployed to a hot spot, which thankfully he was never really sure of till Shane was home, but he hoped that this time would be just like all the others and his brother would be home soon safe and sound.

"I'm here. Gotta go. I'll call when I can, but thanks. For everything."

"You got it, bro. Any time, every time." They'd had each other's backs their whole lives, no point in changing that now.

Tapping in the number for his best friend and coworker, Kent waited for the phone to be answered.

"Hey, man. What's up?"

"How do you feel about sunshine, sunshine and more sunshine?"

"Say again."

"The Caribbean, sand and water. What do you say?"

"Did you drink your lunch today or something?" Jim was a smart guy but sometimes he was just a bit slow on the uptake.

"No. Shane has to cancel his trip so I am now the proud tourist looking for a travel buddy."

"Sold."

"Don't you want to know exactly where we're going? Or for how long?"

"Nope." He could almost hear his friend shaking his head. "Anywhere that isn't here is fine with me and after the week we've had, the longer the better. When are we leaving?"

"Saturday."

"This Saturday?"

"Yep. Can't make it?"

"Are you kidding? I've had it up to my eyeballs with Mother Nature's constant play dates with winter. I'm in."

"Great. Will call later when I have everything set up. Oh, and text me your passport number. I'm going to need it to change the reservations."

"Will do right now."

"Perfect. I can feel the sun baking on my back already."

Jim laughed. "Just remember to roll over."

He'd have to remember a lot of things, but for now, not much else mattered. He was taking a vacation. An honest to goodness, unplug and unwind vacation. And if it went as well as he expected, he might just run away from home for real and never come back.

CHAPTER TWO

"**I** can't believe I'm actually taking a cruise." Mina's youngest sister was grinning so wide Mina wouldn't be surprised if her face froze the way her mother always threatened it would.

"Wow." Her neck craned looking out the transfer bus window, Ginnie's eyes were as round as her open mouth. "That boat is bigger than some cities."

"Ship. You can put a boat on a ship but not a ship on a boat," Mina corrected, silently agreeing with her sister. The ship might not be a city, but it was certainly bigger than some buildings she'd been in. "No wonder people don't get seasick anymore, or at least not as much. That thing is huge."

The bus pulled into a designated parking spot in front of the massive vessel. One by one the sisters descended, following the other tourists awaiting their bags to be removed from the bus and handed off to the porters.

"Maybe we should at least keep our carry-ons?" Jo asked. "I mean, just in case something gets lost."

Mina waved her arm at all the luggage and all the people. "I'm thinking that the ship staff has this thing figured out and our luggage will be perfectly fine. If we can't check into our rooms for a couple more hours, I'm not lugging any luggage all around this ship."

Both sisters nodded at her and followed the lines into the building.

"And I thought the security lines at the airport were long." Jo paused at the signage by the entry to the registration area and pointed to the one that directed the top tier loyalty passengers to the shorter line. "I wonder how many cruises a person has to take to qualify for the faster lines?"

"More than one. Keep going." Ginny nudged her sister forward.

Finally at the front of the line, facing a long row of staff like tellers in a bank, one woman raised her arm, waving them over. "May I see your passports, please?"

Each of them handed over their passports and the miscellaneous paperwork they had been asked to fill out.

Working with practiced efficiency, the woman handed them each a key card, explained some preliminary rules about what could and couldn't be used with the card and plastering on a smile, wished them a pleasant trip.

"Well, that was awfully easy." Jo followed the passengers in front of them. "I didn't say anything, but I was a little worried the last minute change of adding me to the room wasn't going to take and I was going to have to turn around and fly back home."

"Oh, nonsense." Mina rolled her eyes. "Same as with the luggage, these ocean liners have been handling the masses for decades. Everything runs like a well-oiled machine."

"Slow." Ginnie looked at the long security line. "But well-oiled."

The three took the standard pose in front of the big poster photograph. No doubt there would be a lot of those photos over the next seven days.

"Wonder how much they charge for those." At the top of the gangway, Ginnie popped her card into the machine as instructed and hearing the ding, stepped onto the ship.

"More than any of us are probably going to want to pay." Answering her sister, Jo did the same and followed Ginnie onto the ship and through a second security point.

"Okay." Mina stood at the elevator doors reading the ship's map. "Where do we start?"

"Food." Jo grinned at her older sister. "I'm starving."

"You did nothing but eat the entire flight." Ginnie stared slack jaw at her sister. "You polished off all of your breakfast, half of my breakfast, and a blueberry muffin the lady across the aisle didn't want to eat. How could you be hungry?"

Jo shrugged. "I can't help it if I have a fast metabolism. It's after noon, and a perfectly respectable hour to be eating."

Before Ginnie could respond, Mina held up her hand. "I'm a little hungry too. It doesn't look like the main restaurant is open while we're still docked. I can't tell about other snack areas on ship, so it looks like the buffet wins."

Ginnie nodded. "But after that I want to walk around a little, and there's supposed to be a band on deck playing as we shove off. I wonder if they throw streamers and things like the old movies."

"Doubt it, but it will be fun anyhow." Mina grinned at her sister. Stepping into the glass elevator and looking at the different levels as they rode up to the very top had excitement gurgling deep inside her. Until now the whole whirlwind, last minute honeymoon substitution, rush to get ready hadn't given the reality of it all time to sink in. Surrounded by the lights and people of this floating hotel brought reality to life big time. "This is going to be so much fun."

"Look." Jo pointed toward the wall of windows to their right. "There's an empty table. I'll grab it and you guys go scope out the food. When you come back I'll go get mine."

"Sounds like a plan." Walking from section to section, taking in all the varieties of precooked and made to order food, plus the eye-catching display of desserts, Mina realized that there'd be no way to count calories on this little vacation. Not to mention she'd need to get reacquainted with the local gym once she got home. But nibbling on a piece of warm cranberry bread as she perused her options, she already knew every single bite was going to be worth next week's sit-ups.

Ginnie dug her spoon into the creamy dessert. "I think this is a tres leches custard or maybe an exotic flan, but what ever it is, this is the most delicious thing I have ever tasted."

"Don't let Mama hear you say that." Jo dug into her

slice of coconut cake. "Mine's okay. I think I'll try yours."

"While you're up," Ginnie waved a spoon at her younger sister, "bring me another."

Mina took the last bite of her bread pudding and remembering her vow not to count calories, wiggled her fingers at Jo. "I'll try one too."

"We really need to bring Mom on one of these. As much as she loves to cook, I think she'd be thrilled to just eat decadent desserts for a week that she didn't have to bake."

"I don't believe that for a minute. Our mother would last one meal, maybe two, before she's in the kitchen back there showing them how to make things her way."

Ginnie almost spit out her food trying not to laugh. "You may have a point there. I don't know how I could've said anything quite so foolish."

"Here you go." Jo set the dessert in front of her sisters. "I was just chatting with a nice lady who sails a lot with this line. I mentioned that if this is as good as you say it is I might be eating it every opportunity, and she told me that they rotate their desserts so if we find something we really like we need to eat a lot of it as we may not get it again."

Mina dipped her spoon into the creamy dessert, took one taste, and decided her sister was absolutely correct—it was something her mother most definitely would be stealing the recipe for, and if the rest of the cruise had more desserts like this, they were going to be rolling her off this boat. But what a way to go.

"I wonder how many people will be up here before breakfast." Kent and his friend Jim had eaten, toured the ship, and now accompanied by the sounds of a steel band while waiting for the ship to sail, were walking the track on the upper deck. He really liked the idea of having his morning run with a warm breeze and an ocean view. As long as all the people they were now wading through were not going to be early risers as well.

Jim took a swig of his cold beer. "I'm going to take a wild guess that jogging at the crack of dawn isn't top ten on the tourist list of things to do on a cruise ship."

"I hope you're right."

"What you're probably going to have to fight for is a deck chair." Jim waved his finger at the lounge chairs to one side, and the people already staking their claim and soaking up the sun. "I wonder how many of these ladies are single."

The thought had crossed Kent's mind as well. Since his job had shifted to letting those who could work from home do so, instead of cutting down on his hours, it turned out that more often than not, working from the comfort of his own home, he'd found himself still on the computer way after shutting down time. He'd also found that the boundaries for after hour data checks were slipping away as the requests for after hours data runs were coming in more and more frequently. All of which meant his love life had taken a hit. What he wasn't quite sure of is whether or not a shipboard flirtation was just the ticket or a really bad idea. Only time would tell.

As they came around the back of the ship, Jim slowed his pace. "Nine o'clock. Check it out."

It took Kent a few long seconds to recognize that his buddy was not referring to the time, or a schedule, but the direction to their right just about where the number nine would be on a clock. What he had to figure out was exactly what was he looking at.

"I think this is just as good a spot as any to stop and enjoy the show when the ship pulls out."

And now Kent knew what Jim had zeroed in on. Several feet ahead and to his left, three women stood at the rail, laughing and clearly enjoying the moment. Of course, he doubted what had caught Jim's eye was their good mood. Knowing his friend's taste, he was going to guess it was the blonde with her hair in a ponytail that had Jim veering left like a magnet to true north.

On either side of the blonde were two brunettes. One wore a large floppy hat with sunglasses almost as big as her face, making it hard to see if there was any family resemblance. The other woman did not look anything like the blonde. While they stood about the same height, the blonde had on high heeled sandals and the brunette wore flats. But what struck him wasn't her height, or how the almost auburn highlights in her chestnut colored hair shone in the sun, or that unlike the rail thin build that most modern women strived for, she had old fashioned curves. What had his attention was the smile. Not just any smile. A broad grin that came with a deep rumbling laugh. The kind that made him want to know what was so funny.

Jim stopped a few feet away and Kent leaned against the railing beside him, happy to simply watch the ladies for a few minutes and bask in their happy moods. Their plan for after the ship set sail was to head to the cabin and change for dinner. They had considered stopping in their room earlier to make sure their luggage had arrived but figured it could wait. After all, if the luggage hadn't arrived, there wasn't anything knowing about it sooner could change about it. Besides, soaking in the vacation atmosphere of live music, warm weather, and people watching was much more inviting than unpacking. Especially watching one *people* in particular.

The ship's horn blew and the blonde squealed, "We're moving!"

"I would hope so," the brunette with the infectious smile poked fun at her friend. "Certainly wouldn't want to spend my week parked here."

"Agreed." The one with the floppy hat raised a fruity drink in a mock toast. "Though I have a feeling being on this boat for a week parked just about anywhere beats my office hands down and then some."

Jim shifted his stance and making eye contact with the blonde, smiled. "Is this your first cruise?"

The blonde bobbed her head up and down. "For me and my sisters."

Ah, so they *were* related. Funny how some families, like him and his brother who were clearly chips off of his father's block, were instantly recognizable as related, and yet others like these three, not so much.

"This is my first cruise too." Jim stretched out his hand. "I'm Jim. This is my buddy, Kent."

"Nice to meet you." The blonde was doing all the talking, the two brunettes were just watching. "I'm Jo. These are my sisters, Ginnie and Mina."

Kent wasn't sure which was which since Jo hadn't actually pointed to anyone.

"We probably should head to our room." The sister with the floppy hat stepped away from the rail. "Make sure our luggage got to the right cabin and all."

"Good idea." The other brunette nodded before glancing in their direction. "It was nice meeting you. Enjoy your trip."

"You too." Kent was sorely tempted to add see you around but decided the way the two sisters whisked Jo away, it wouldn't have been well received.

Jim shrugged and turned to Kent. "We might as well do the same. Maybe we'll have better luck over dinner."

They turned in the opposite direction the ladies had gone, crossed the pool deck and caught the elevator down to their floor.

"I wonder if we'll bump into them again." Jim stepped out onto their deck level.

"It's a big ship." A little too big to get lucky enough to run into the ladies again. Too bad. They turned the corner into the hallway and he kept his gaze on the door numbers.

"922, 924, here we are." He stopped in front of the door to 926 and thought his luck had to be improving as the three women came from the opposite end of the hall, counting doors the same as they had just done.

"Hello again." Jim waved. "I guess we're on the same deck. What a nice coincidence."

Holding her hat in her hand, the one sister smiled awkwardly, her gaze shifting from them to the door and back.

"I guess it's a big ship but a small world." Jo smiled. A nice smile, but nothing like her sisters.

"Yes. And if you gentlemen will excuse us." The

brunette, whose name he wished he knew, moved in front of the other two sisters holding up her card. "We want to unpack before dinner."

"Yes." Kent nodded at her. "That's our plan too."

Just as he turned to slide the key into the door lock, his brunette turned and bumped shoulders with him. "Excuse me."

Looking from her to their hands extended in front of the door, and back to her again, the frown that had settled between her brows matched the confusion taking up his thoughts.

"We're in room 926," she said firmly.

"So are we." Kent held up the card.

His brunette shook her head. "That's not possible." She held up her card. "This is our cabin." Without giving him a minute to answer, she shoved the card into the door and dipping the handle, pushed the door open, then turned to him smiling. "See?"

Just to make sure he hadn't lost his mind, he looked at his card to confirm he hadn't read it wrong. "I don't know about this." Grabbing the handle of the door, he pulled it shut, stuck his key in the slot and pushing on the handle the same way she had, shoved the door open. "And in those infamous words, 'Houston, we have a problem'."

CHAPTER THREE

None of this made any sense, and having a good-looking stranger breathing down her neck was not helping Mina's thought process. Standing in the small room, surrounded by her sisters and two strangers, she looked around. First thing she noticed was that even if there hadn't been a room mix-up, this cabin only had two beds. No place for the third sister. The next thing she noticed was with luggage for five people there wasn't much room for anyone to move, never mind relax. What she really wanted right now more than anything was to get these guys out of their cabin. "This just can't be."

"I'm sure there's an easy fix." The man with steel gray eyes that made her mouth go dry turned to his buddy. "Let's hit the concierge and get this sorted out."

Mina nodded and slipping her key into her pocket, looked to her sisters. "You can wait here in our room. I'll go take care of this."

"Nope." Ginnie shook her head. "You can still do all the talking, but we stick together."

"Yes," Jo nodded, "you're good at that, but I'm with Ginnie. We all go."

"Okay." Mina led the way out the door and down the hall. "I simply don't understand how this could happen."

"Do you think it's because of the last minute name change?" Jo inched up beside her sister. "We didn't give them much notice."

Kent called from behind Ginnie, "You changed your reservation at the last minute?"

"That's right." Mina nodded.

"So did we." Jim frowned from the rear. "I wonder how

many other passengers with last minute reservations are in the wrong cabin."

"And I didn't see anywhere for a third bed." Jo blew out a deep sigh. "Did you?"

Shaking her head, Mina picked up the pace. If this was a sign of how the rest of the vacation would go, it was definitely going to be a bumpy ride. No one said another word. The glass elevators that had been so intriguing on the previous rides up and down now felt very, very small. They exited the elevator, and came to a halt at the end of a too long line.

Jim shook his head. "I was only kidding when I said all the last minute reservations were botched, but now I wonder."

"They couldn't possibly have messed up all these people's rooms." Kent's gaze moved from each of the three agents at the counter to all the passengers standing in front of them.

"Thank heaven it's a big ship. How hard can it be to shuffle a few people around?" Ginnie cracked a smile. She was right. This couldn't be the first or last time someone's reservations were messed up. The desk agents had to be used to this. All would be fixed in a few minutes. She hoped.

Several of the people ahead of them had easy issues. A few just wanted schedules or something equally simple because they barely stood in front of the agent before walking away with papers in hand. The woman directly in front of them was waved over and Mina could hear her complaining about not receiving her luggage. She couldn't help but wish that her problem had been that simple. Deep in her nervous gut a small voice shouted *don't unpack, they're going to ship you home.*

"They're calling us." Kent reached for her elbow and then quickly pulled his arm back. "Let's get this settled."

Taking the lead, it took Mina only a few minutes to describe their dilemma. The petite woman in a dark blue suit shook her head. "That's not possible. Let me see your keys."

Four more keys landed on the counter beside Mina's.

"You'll see." Kent tapped the counter with his finger. "All have the same cabin number on them."

The frown on the petite woman's face grew deeper as she examined each key.

Mina's nervous gut started doing somersaults. She didn't like that frown one bit. She didn't like any of this one bit.

Shaking her head, the agent muttered, "this is not possible," as she tapped her keyboard some more then looked up. "Which one of you is Mr. Harwood?"

At the same time Mina responded, "he's not here," Kent inched closer to the counter and his words "I am" colliding with hers.

She spun about to face him. "Your name is Harwood?" This was all going from crazy to downright insane.

Kent nodded. "The reservations were originally my brother's but his unit was deployed unexpectedly so he and his wife—"

"Had to cancel," Mina finished the sentence for him. "Melody gave us their reservation."

"Why would she give you the cabin if Shane gave us the cabin?"

"I would guess Shane and Melody both had the same idea. We appear to be suffering from a gross case of spousal failure to communicate." She narrowed her gaze looking into steely eyes. "Were you at the wedding?"

He nodded.

"I don't remember seeing you."

"He shaved." Jim laughed. "Told him to do it before the wedding photos. That his new sister-in-law would appreciate it, but it took the threat of a tropical heat wave to get him to do it. He cleans up pretty good."

The brother rolled his eyes and returning his attention to the desk agent, ignored his buddy's teasing. Mina remembered the best man had a beard. He also had a lovely fashionable blonde on his arm so she didn't give him another glance.

The petite agent lifted her gaze from the keyboard,

following their conversation with interest.

Kent focused on the agent. "Do you think that all of us changing the reservation at the same time could be why they allowed five us to be booked in one room?"

"That's impossible." The woman shook her head and continued clacking on the keyboard.

The look on Kent's face grew in intensity, his tone dropping a smidge lower, he enunciated very clearly, "Obviously it is possible because we're holding five key cards to a two bed cabin."

"I'm telling you," the lady repeated, "it's impossible for our computer system to double book one room. Even if human error was involved, the computer would catch the error and correct it."

"I paid for the third bed," Jo put in.

"And you are?" the woman asked.

Jo inched closer and lowered her voice. "Josephine Ummarino."

All the sisters got saddled with traditional Italian names. And all three of them went by nicknames not their given names, but Jo was the only one who absolutely hated her Italian name and wasn't overjoyed with the English translation. Most people knew her as Jo or Josephine and didn't have a clue what her real name was.

Continuing to clack away at the keyboard, the woman's frown deepened, not at all helping to make Mina feel any more secure about this being resolved easily.

Another staff person in a white shirt came up behind the agent helping them. "I need a cabin. What have you got going?"

"Kennel booking."

Kent's brow raised and he turned to face his friend as Mina looked to her sister. No doubt he was thinking the same thing she was. If they had a nickname for this, it surely wasn't the oddity the woman insisted it was.

The other lady pressed her lips tightly before speaking. "Toilet in 521 is irreparable. We need to move them."

"We're booked solid. I'm checking no shows now." The agent shook her head and the lady in white frowned more deeply while looking over the agent's shoulder at the screen.

Turning his back to the counter, Kent leaned into the sisters. "If I'm putting two and two together correctly, they don't have an extra room for us and now there's another passenger with no place to sleep either."

The beginnings of a nasty headache were drumming at Mina's temple. "I'm not looking forward to sleeping in the life rafts."

Kent chuckled softly. "I doubt it will come to that. This ship has to be like any other hotel or theater. They always save space for last minute VIPs."

"From your mouth to God's ears," Ginnie muttered.

The first thing Kent wanted to know was why the heck his brother and sister-in-law both gave away the cabin. If this was the way they communicated as married people, the next few years were going to be doozies.

"Okay." The woman stopped attacking her keyboard and looked up at them. "The ship is completely full. Operations is doing a confirmation to see if all passengers checked in."

Overhead, as the woman spoke, names were being called and he wondered if those were people with missing luggage, missing companions, or the no-shows the liner was hoping for.

"As soon as we have a correct head count, we'll be able to move one of you out of the room and into your own rooms."

He had to give the lady, all the ladies, credit. Most of the women he knew would have been raising cane by now. Except for the occasional hands moving about as they spoke, these gals seemed awfully calm and reserved. If he was a guessing man, he'd venture that Mina was the first born and took her responsibilities as big sister seriously.

"How long will that take?" Mina asked.

"Not much longer." The woman returned to her keyboard. The frown kept coming and going. Kent had no clue if the disconcerted expression had anything to do with them, or the poor people with the broken toilet or something totally unrelated.

Mina addressed her sisters. "If you guys want to go out on deck and see what's happening, I can wait here."

Both shook their heads, but Ginnie answered. "Sticking close by will be easier than tracking us down when this is all straightened out."

From the sour expressions on everyone's faces, he wasn't as confident as Ginnie that this situation would indeed get sorted out.

The two women behind the counter began chattering again, too softly for him to clearly make out what they were saying, but while their agent shook her head, the other woman pointed to the screen and finally the woman who had been typing almost nonstop sighed and smiled up at them. "It looks like we have a solution."

He really hoped it was going to be good news and that none of them would be sleeping poolside on deck chairs, or worse catching a tug boat back to port.

"We don't have access to the reservation data base so we have no idea what went wrong."

Everyone nodded. And if they did they probably would never admit it anyhow.

"Usually there are spare rooms for upgrades and other situations."

As he'd suspected.

"But not today."

And now was where the part Mina had mentioned about deck chairs came into play.

"We've only had one no show. Your assigned cabin can't hold all of you and we need it for the other displaced passenger, so we're going to have to move you all to the honeymoon suite."

"All of us?" He knew that suites were bigger than regular rooms, but he couldn't imagine it being big enough for five people. Especially when half of them didn't know the other half.

For the first time since they first expressed their dilemma, the woman smiled brightly. "It's a two bedroom suite. You'll have your own deck and the suite comes with a hot tub."

"The honeymoon suite has two bedrooms?" Mina asked the same question he was wondering.

"It used to be one of the Presidential Suites but when they redesigned the ship a few years ago, they absorbed some of the other suites to create family entertainment space so this one was renamed the Honeymoon Suite." The agent handed them each a new gold colored card. "The attendants will move your luggage. If you need anything else, just let us know."

An awkward silence surrounded them as they stepped away from the counter.

"Do you think we're going to be charged more money for this?" Jo held up her keycard.

Jim was quick to shake his head. "Absolutely not. This was their screw up."

"Well," for the first time since he'd seen Mina and her sisters laughing on deck, the smile was back, "shall we go check out our new home?"

"This could be fun." Jo smiled and pushed the button for the elevator. "Haven't shared a place with this many people since college."

"Mm," was all Mina said. Ginnie cast a sideways glance in her sisters' direction.

He got the definite impression that Ginnie and Mina were the more serious side of the family.

"I wonder if they've got any chianti on this boat?" Ginnie waited behind her sisters as Kent slid the keycard into the door.

He shoved it open and waved the women in first.

"Holy..." Jo stood in the middle of the room turning three hundred and sixty degrees. Unlike the cabin they'd just left, the room was not only huge, the ceilings were twice as high, making the suite feel as big as a ballroom. Large leather seating was precisely placed around the open space for both style and comfort. A few tables and chairs were dispersed for meals or game time or whatever else the passengers saw fit to do with them. She didn't know which was more stunning, the sleek chrome accents and fixtures or the expansive wall of glass separating them from the outdoors. Still spinning slowly, she spotted the tray of chocolate covered strawberries on the coffee table and quickly snatched one up and took a bite. Savoring the decadent fruit with a soft moan, she held the half-eaten berry up for her sisters to see. "I have a feeling this is going to be the best five hundred and forty dollars I have ever spent."

A knock from the open door sounded behind him and a porter brought in their luggage. "Here are your bags. Which ones go in which room?"

Kent looked from the bags to the man and noticed all the doors in the suite. "Just leave them right there. We'll move them later."

The man nodded and unloaded the bags. "Your regular steward will be by shortly to assist you with anything else you might need."

"Thank you," a few voices echoed.

The moment the door latched shut behind the porter, Jo hurried to the closest door in the front bedroom and looked inside. "Not bad."

"This one's nice too." Ginnie bobbed her head, coming out of the other bedroom. "Very nice."

"I'm not particular." Jim was already standing behind the bar. "This thing is fully stocked. I wonder if it's on the house or just an oversized and expensive version of a mini bar."

Mina had gone from room to room. "We'll take the room with the two queens. You guys can have the king."

"Sounds good." Kent didn't mind sharing a bed under the right circumstances, but he wasn't so sure Jim was it. Hopefully the guy stuck to his own side.

"As long as I don't have to share with Jo. She does gymnastics in her sleep."

"I do not." Jo stared pointedly at her sister.

"You're also a cover hog. I feel sorry for your husband when you get married. He'll be sound asleep only to find himself woken up by a flying arm in the face or foot in the gut."

"That's not true." Now Jo was frowning at her sister.

"Sure it is. I will never forget the time when we were kids and spent the night at Nonna's. She put you and me in the same bed. In the middle of the night you put your feet against my back and shoved me onto the floor."

"That's right." Mina laughed. "I was on the sofa in the living room and the thud woke me out of a sound sleep."

"See?" Ginnie waved a triumphant arm at her sister and Kent did his best to bite back a laugh.

"If no one else wants to share with you…" From behind the bar, Jim looked to Jo and let his words fall off. It took one look from Kent for him to wave a hand at his new roommates. "Only kidding."

From the sour expression on Mina's face, she didn't find the comment all that amusing either.

"Well, at least I don't talk in my sleep!"

Both Mina and her sister Ginnie sputtered like used cars with bad gas. "I do not," tumbled over, "I never!" This little discussion was proving more entertaining than a late night comedy sketch.

"What about the time that we stayed up late watching that old Al Pacino movie about a crooked judge and in the middle of the night, Ginnie sat up straight and yelled, 'I abstain!' Scared the dickens out of all of us. She yelled so loud, Mama came running up the hall."

"Well," Ginnie waved a dismissive hand in the air, "one unsettling movie and bad Chinese food."

At this point, both Mina and Jim were biting their lower lips to keep their mouths shut and Kent was wondering if maybe the next few days weren't going to be quite as peaceful as he'd projected.

"You two can share the bed, I'll pick up earplugs at one of the shops." Jo spun around and took a step toward the far side of the room before looking over her shoulder. "And I don't steal the covers!" Practically storming across the living space, she opened the patio door and marched out onto the deck. "Oh, my. The lady wasn't kidding when she said our own deck. It's huge."

Curious, Kent crossed the room to see, Ginnie on his heels.

"It's as big out here as it is in there." Ginnie stood in the middle of the deck and spun around, a huge grin taking over her face. "This is way cool. Maybe we should just sleep out here?"

Kent considered the situation. He and his buddy were about to share a rather spacious and luxurious suite with three beautiful women they barely knew. At least two of whom seemed less than pleased with him and Jim as roommates. He wasn't so sure 'cool' was the best description. As far as he was concerned, interesting was a better word, and whether or not that was a good or bad thing was yet to be determined.

CHAPTER FOUR

"**T**his whole thing is too weird for words." Even something as ordinary as unpacking had become a surreal experience with a closet bigger than Mina's entire bedroom at home. "Never mind that we are sharing our living space with two strange men."

"They're not strange." Jo closed the drawer she'd just filled from her suitcase. "Kent is Shane's brother, and we know Shane is a nice guy."

"I'm sure Abel was a nice guy too but that didn't stop his brother Cain from killing him." Mina set her empty bag on the top shelf and closed the closet door behind her.

"Oh, come on." Ginnie slipped on her comfy sandals. "That's a little extreme even for you. Don't you think?"

Mina shook her head. "Okay, I'll give you that he's probably not a murderer, but it's still very weird sharing where we live and sleep with men we don't know."

"At least they've been downgraded from strange to unknown." Jo slipped out of her shorts and into a sundress. "I think they're nice."

Ginnie nodded. "Considering we were all thrown for a loop, they did take it well."

"What's hard to take?" Jo stood at the open terrace door. "This place is bigger than my first apartment, and who doesn't like chocolate covered strawberries and champagne."

"Champagne?" Mina turned to her sister. "What champagne?"

"There's a bottle chilling on the bar."

"Really?" Ginnie smiled. "I didn't notice."

"Do you think they'll bring strawberries every night?"

Jo smoothed away some of the luggage wrinkles from her dress.

"I doubt it."

"Well," Jo beamed at her sisters, "I'm starved. Where to now?"

Her sister was right. Hours had passed since they'd had lunch and the desserts may have been heavenly, but they weren't the hearty foods that would sustain a person for long. "Let's hit the dining room. We can check out our other dinner options for the rest of the cruise later."

"Sounds good." Ginnie nodded. "Let's go."

"Should we check on what the boys are doing?" Jo followed her sister into the living area.

"Boys?" Mina would describe them in many ways. Handsome came to mind, but boys did not. "We may be sharing a suite but we are not sharing our vacation."

They'd barely made it out the bedroom door when they came smack dab in contact with Jim at the bar.

Jim opened a canister of chips. "I really think I could get to like this place."

"You'll spoil your dinner," Mina said without thinking.

He chuckled, and the sound of a door unlatching across the room had all three looking up.

"Nothing could spoil that man's dinner." Dressed in khakis and a clean shirt, his hair still wet from a shower, Kent crossed the room to the bar. "But it is dinner time and I'm starting to feel hungry."

"Are you guys hitting the dining room or the buffet again?" Jo was for sure the most extroverted of the sisters. Not that Mina and Ginnie were introverts, they were far from it. Mina wasn't even sure if it was possible to be raised Italian and be an introvert, but Jo always had a friendly smile and kind word for any soul. These guys could turn out to be the biggest jerks, and Jo would still do her best to make nice. Mina, on the other hand, was a realist. And she was really hoping that Shane's brother and his friend weren't going to cause any trouble.

"Actually," Jim was the more relaxed of the two, "we're heading to the dining room."

"Good." Jo smiled brightly. "We'll walk with you."

Jim and Jo led the way, leaning into each other, chatting softly, and laughing from time to time.

"Looks like they're connecting," Ginnie whispered softly, tipping her head in her sister's direction.

The same thing had crossed Mina's mind. "Better keep an eye on them." Not that her sister wasn't a big girl, but her track record with men wasn't stellar and they didn't really know squat about Jim. Mina had watched over her kid sisters her whole life; now didn't seem like the time to change that up. She and Kent were the two on the tail end of the single file line down the hall to the elevators.

"Have you been on a cruise before?" Kent asked from behind her.

She shook her head, keeping one eye on her youngest sister while holding up her end of the conversation.

In the elevator, no one had to say anything as Jim and Jo were doing just fine at filling everyone in on their interests and commonalities.

"Looks like we're not the only ones who are hungry." Ginnie stopped at the long line by the dining room.

"It's only the first night," Kent reassured.

Mina turned to him. "You've cruised before?"

"A couple of times. Once on this line and once on the party line."

"Party line?" Ginnie laughed. "Sounds like an old telephone hookup."

Kent chuckled quietly. "Cruise lines are all noted for different things. I tried them both and the other cruise company caters to young party people and while I enjoy a good time as much as the next guy, this line is more of a happy medium."

"Good to know." Mina nodded and as an after thought, smiled back at him. She was going to have to work on that. It wasn't Kent or his friend's fault that his brother gave away the same reservation that his sister-in-law gave them, and it wasn't his fault that the cruise line didn't catch the double booking.

"Really?" Jo squealed softly.

Mina had let her mind wander. "Really what?"

"The ship gives scuba diving lessons. We could all get certified and then scuba with the real fish at the last port!"

Jo was way too happy about being trapped underwater. Mina didn't have any objections to swimming in the ocean, but she much preferred sailing on it. Diving under it was not on her bucket list.

"Scuba diving!" Ginnie's tone straddled something between shock and awe.

"Now you sound like Mina." Jo frowned. "I expected push back from the serious sister, but not you."

"Wait a minute." Mina couldn't decide if she should stomp her feet and declare darn straight she was serious, or point out that she could be just as much fun as the next guy. Just not underwater. "Never mind."

"See?" Jo waved at her older sister. "Not an adventurous bone in her body."

"I can be adventurous." Mina had just made up her mind. She did not want to be the stick in the mud sister.

"That'll be the day," Jo mumbled under her breath, then pushed onto her tippy toes and kissed her sister on the cheek. "But we love you just the way you are."

Ginnie nodded agreement with her sister and, in the few moments they stood online together, Mina already decided keeping an eye on Jo would prove to be a full-time assignment. She could hardly wait till her adventurous sister realized that scuba lessons were only the tip of the proverbial iceberg. For those passengers that were not risk averse, the options ranged from rock climbing to parasailing to scuba diving and who knew how much more. Yep, Mina sighed, keeping up with Jo would not be for the faint of heart. The real question was how far was Mina willing to go to keep up.

Getting more than a two word response out of Mina was proving to be a bit of a challenge for Kent. Though he wasn't sure why he was trying so hard. There had to be plenty of women on this ship who would be more than happy to kick up a conversation with him, and yet, there was something about Mina that had him wanting to try harder. He had a feeling there was a lot more to this classic beauty with the hard surface of a protective big sister.

Jo and Jim happily chatted about anything from the menu to the onboard activities for their first day at sea tomorrow. The way that Mina stood stiffly beside her sister suggested she was less than thrilled with the suggestions, or maybe he was over-reading her reactions. Maybe the lady simply had good posture.

"Room cards, please?" The man by the podium glanced at the cards and nodded. "Follow me, please."

Smiling sweetly, Jo waved goodbye to Kent and Jim and followed the man into the formal dining.

"She's nice." Jim kept his gaze on the three women's departing backs.

"They all are, but they're also my brother's neighbors. Please don't do anything that's going to come back and bite me."

"Moi?" Jim's eyes opened wide.

All Kent had to do was glare at him.

"Message received." Holding his hands up in the air palms out, he grinned at his friend. "Promise, hands off."

Considering how well he knew Jim's playful side, he hoped it would be that easy.

A different restaurant staff member looked at their cards and gestured for them to follow. The opulence of the dining rooms on these ships always intrigued him. This floor's dining room decorated in shades of blue, the high drapes on the massive picture windows, the columns throughout, the gold and blue carpet underfoot, as well as the plush crushed velvet seating at all the tables were some of the few things about cruising that lingered from the days of the Titanic and luxury travel.

Busy taking in his surroundings, he almost bumped into the crewman when he came to an unexpected stop. Even more unexpected were the people at the table.

"Hello." An older woman with a hairdo piled on her head that reminded Kent of photos of his grandmother from the fifties, bobbed her head at him.

Beside her, a gentleman glanced up from his menu. "Guess I won't be outnumbered anymore."

"George." The big hair woman smacked the man lightly on his arm.

"No offense, dear." The man leaned over and kissed his wife sweetly on her cheek before looking up at him. "I'm George Findley. This is my wife Susan and my daughter Jennifer."

"Kent Harwood."

"Jim Stone."

From the other side of the large table, Jo grinned and waved with her fingers. "Isn't this a nice surprise?"

Jim took the available chair beside Jo, leaving Kent in the seat across from Mina.

"We're so happy to be here," Susan beamed, "after putting the trip off twice I didn't think we were ever going to take this vacation."

"Is it your first cruise?" Mina asked.

Susan shook her head. "Oh, heavens no. We've been cruising for years. And you?"

"It's our first time," Mina confirmed.

"We tried to get our other daughters and their families to join us, but it didn't work out this time."

"Could you imagine if we brought our entire family?" Jo rolled her eyes.

"Oy." Ginnie waved one hand in the air. "Once Mama was done showing the chef's how to really cook, she'd probably move on to telling the captain how to drive the boat!"

Mina chuckled. "You know she'd spend all her time in the kitchn."

"Your mother likes to cook?" Susan asked.

"Is the Pope Catholic?" Ginnie deadpanned.

Susan and her husband laughed while their daughter quietly watched the banter like a spectator at a tennis match.

By the time they'd gotten through dinner, he'd learned

Susan and George were the proud parents of four girls. Three grown and married and he suspected Jennifer had been a later in life surprise. He'd also been taken aback to learn the girls' full non-anglicized names. If he hadn't already known they were Italian, names like Philomena, Giovanna, and Giuseppina, not Joanna or Josephine, would certainly have given their ancestry away.

"Can I really?" For the first time all evening, Jennifer seemed actually excited about something. The only problem, Kent had lost track of the conversation.

"Oh," Susan frowned, "I don't know."

"Daddy, please?"

"It will be perfectly safe," Jo reassured. On the other hand, Mina and Ginnie looked almost as disconcerted as Mrs. Findley.

"Daddy?"

"Well." Looking from his wife frowning at him to his daughter's puppy dog eyes, Kent could read the conflict poor George battled. Blowing out a slow sigh and reaching over to squeeze his wife's hand, George nodded. "I suppose if Miss Ummarino is going to try it and if the ship says it's all right, then it's all right with me, but we'll have to see about diving in the actual ocean."

Ahh. Now he got it. Jo hadn't forgotten about the scuba certification and apparently she'd roped Jennifer into taking classes with her, but not so much her sisters.

"George?"

"It will be fine, Susan."

The poor woman didn't look convinced but George was right. Learning to dive in the ship's pool was probably the safest place to learn.

"Time for music trivia." George set his napkin aside, swallowed the last sip of his wine, and pushed away from the table. "Tonight is Elvis night. You folks want to join us? Susan and I know our Elvis but there's safety in numbers."

The three sisters looked at each other, one raised a brow, another made a funny move with her mouth and in the end they all nodded.

"You gentlemen?"

Before Jim could enthusiastically agree to make nice some more with Jo, Kent spoke up. "Maybe another night. We've got a casino to check out."

As they stood to leave the table, he thought he saw disappointment flash in Mina's eyes. Weaving past the tables on their way out, listening to her chatter merrily with Susan and Jennifer, he decided his observations were nothing more than hopeful thinking. And why did he even care?

CHAPTER FIVE

"We're only on day two of this trip and I already feel like a turkey on Thanksgiving." Ginnie pushed back from the table.

Jo patted her stomach. "You're right but it is so worth it. I don't know which was better, the eggs benedict or the sugar crepes."

"All I know is if they keep feeding us like this they're going to have to roll me off this ship in a wheel barrow." Having been raised in an Italian household, Mina was no stranger to good food, but this never ending supply of delicious cuisine was definitely a threat to her waistline.

"I'm going to walk off some of this hearty meal before the scuba class." Jo looked around the room. "I'm supposed to meet Jennifer in twenty minutes. Any of you guys change your mind and want to join us?"

"I'm already certified, thanks."

Mina whirled around to face Kent. "You are?"

He nodded. "Don't look so surprised."

"Sorry." She had no idea why that startled her. She supposed that deep down she assumed only people who lived near the ocean had an interest in diving. Silly assumption, but it made her wonder what else was under the surface of this man.

"I'm afraid I have a very important lunch date." Jim smiled at his roommates.

"Lunch?" Kent's brows practically touched his hairline. "We just had breakfast."

"Yes." Jim nodded. "I know that, and you know that, but the pretty little blonde from the casino last night does not."

Kent rolled his eyes and shrugged. "Have fun."

"That's the plan." Jim winked at his buddy and Mina had the feeling she wasn't going to be seeing all that much of her fifth roommate this trip after all.

"So," Ginnie smiled at them, "rumba lessons or the game room?"

Jo frowned. "I want to take the rumba lessons. They have another session this afternoon. Why don't you guys go play games and we'll all meet after lunch for the rumba lessons."

Mina looked to her other sister.

"Fine with me if it's fine with you." Ginnie shrugged, and turned to Kent. "Up for a friendly card game or do you have other plans too?"

Shifting his weight from one foot to the other, the way Kent looked over their shoulders, Mina thought he was looking for a way to back out of joining them, but to her surprise, he smiled and nodded. "Sounds like fun."

Up a few decks, they found the game room and way more people than Mina had expected. The way the deck chairs overflowed with sun-worshipping passengers, she hadn't expected to find so many people playing cards.

"Looks like we're not on our own." Glancing around at all the people already set up in place with their games of choice, Mina considered their options. "Cards or board game?"

Ginnie shrugged. Kent waved his arms. "I'll do whatever."

One table caught her eye. It was one of only a few larger roundtables that seated eight not six or four, and three places were empty. "That table there has a larger group, could be more interesting."

Kent and Ginnie both nodded.

It took an extra ounce of willpower not to look down at Kent's hand when he placed it at the small of her back to lead the way, maneuvering through the miscellaneous tables and chairs. One gentleman at the table shuffled a deck of cards while another opened a second deck.

Kent glanced at the other players. "Are these seats taken?"

"Do you play poker?" The man shuffling cards was in his mid forties with salt and pepper hair. A deep voice raised one brow waiting for a response.

Having absolutely no clue if Kent played, Mina gave him a sideways glance and whispered, "Do you?"

A hint of a smile graced his lips. "A little."

Keeping her voice low, Mina leaned into his side. "I haven't played since I was a kid, I probably won't be any good."

"It's all in fun," he whispered back. "I don't think anyone's looking for a championship game." He pulled a seat back for her and smiled at the others. "Sounds like we're in."

For whatever reason, the deep voiced man looked less than thrilled and the brunette at his side must have noticed the same thing because she rammed a not so casual elbow into his side. The guy sputtered, clearing his throat, and plastered on a smile that reminded Mina more of a sneering predator about to enjoy his next meal. "I'm Jake. Glad to have you."

The other folks at the table introduced themselves and the grumpy one, Jake, dealt the first hand. "Five card stud, nothing wild, we don't play like a bunch of sissies."

"Jake." Once again, the brunette elbowed him.

"I'm just saying, this is a real man's game."

This time the woman settled for rolling her eyes. Next, Jake opened a small case that at a quick glance resembled a travel chess or checkers set. Inside instead was a colorful assortment of undersized poker chips and Mina wondered what had they gotten themselves into.

Staring at the box, Kent snapped his jaw closed when he felt Mina lean in closer. "Maybe this was a mistake? Even at eight I wasn't all that good at cards."

"It's just a game," Kent reassured her—and himself. "Just a game."

First round, everyone antied up, five cards dealt, and he couldn't decide what to do with the mishmash he'd been dealt. Discarding two cards, he watched as Ginnie did the same. Mina stared stone-faced at the cards. Kent had no idea if she didn't have a clue what was going on, or if she had a superb poker face. In the end, he and two others were out and it was Jake, Mina, and a nice enough fellow named Joe who had said very little.

He kept his gaze on Mina, waiting.

"Three ladies." Jake laid his cards on the table. Even though his facial expression didn't change, Kent could see the satisfied gleam in his eyes.

"Beats me. Pair of deuces and fives." Joe tossed his hand onto the growing pile of cards.

Like Jake, Mina's expression hadn't changed but he could see the smile in her eyes. "Looks like this one's mine, fellas." Neatly spread out in front of her were three tens and two jacks.

Next round, the brunette at Jake's side dealt the cards. Lady Luck was not any kinder to Kent this time around. Either he kept the pair of deuces or the three hearts. Neither was very hopeful. When his turn came, he opted to try for the flush and discarded two cards. To his left, Mina remained stoic and still. No shuffling about of cards, no telling facial expressions. Just waiting her turn. She asked for one card. The bets increased and the last two players standing, so to speak, were Jake and Mina. Same as the last round, Mina beat Jake's Ace high straight flush and Jake looked less than happy. Kent wasn't too sure what protocol called for, but risked taking a second to stretch his hand to one side and quickly squeeze her hand in his. The slight jump in her seat at the touch of his hand gave away how intently she'd been following the cards and the dealer. When her gaze met his, a brief smile crossed her lips. It was a pretty smile.

"I thought you mentioned you hadn't played since you were a kid?" One of the women at the table cut the deck for the dealer and then smiled back at Mina.

"That's right," Mina replied softly.

The woman hefted a shoulder in a half-hearted shrug. "Then, honey, I suggest you try your luck in the casino after this."

Mina chuckled quietly. "Beginner's luck has to run out eventually."

Beginner's luck was debatable. The next several rounds went pretty much the same way so long as Mina stayed in the game. One hand went to Ginnie and one to Joe. If Mina didn't fold, she won the pot. Her gaze held an almost constant intensity. A concentration. A confidence of when to call, when to bet, when to raise, when to fold, and she hadn't been wrong yet. She most definitely rocked the whole lady luck thing. If he didn't know better, he'd have wagered she was a professional gambler. Then it struck him. Maybe she was. After all, she hadn't said a word so far about what she or her sisters did for a living. Though she had said she hadn't played since she was a kid. He literally shook his head to rattle the crazy thought away.

More hands played, and Mina continued winning. All of a sudden one chair after another began scraping against the tile floors. It was clearly time for other activities to begin. The groups at other tables pushed to their feet and meandered about, laughing and chatting with their newfound friends as they shuffled out of the room. Still in the middle of a round, no one at their table had made any effort to move. Frankly, Kent was pretty sure Jake would have played till they docked back home in an effort to win back his theoretic losses.

"Will we see you at the dance class?" Jennifer's mom set a hand on her shoulder and spoke softly. "My husband has two left feet but one can always hope."

Mina blinked and Kent could almost see her mind flipping from card playing mode to social mode. Another blink and she nodded. "Oh. Yes. Of course."

Almost as an afterthought, her eyes widened and Mina glanced at her cards again.

"Read 'em and weep." Jake laid his cards down. A full house, Jacks over tens.

Mina grinned and closing the cards she held in her

hand, set them face down on the table and pushed away for the table. "Thanks for letting us join you. It was fun."

Together the three of them walked out the game room door, down the short hall, and through the double glass doors onto the deck.

Holding her hands tightly fisted in front of her, Mina stomped her feet quickly and squealed so loud that Kent almost jumped back through the doorway.

"I won," she squealed more loudly. "I never win. Ever."

Her glee was totally contagious. He couldn't have stopped the smile from spreading across his face if his life depended on it. "I thought you said you didn't play?"

Her hand on her heart, her eyes still beaming with delight, leaning against the railing, Mina shook her head. "Not since I was a kid. My grandmother taught me and we would play for hours when I'd visit her. She had a way with cards. Poor Nonno always lost. Though sometimes I thought he did it on purpose just to see my Nonna smile. They were quite the pair. Anyhow, I don't get the chance to play at much of anything, but I never win. Not at rummy, Monopoly, checkers, and I won't mention how many lottery tickets I've bought in adulthood. I never win."

"You certainly made up for it. Today you were definitely the Queen of Hearts."

"Queen of Hearts." Her expression softened. "I like that."

The double doors opened again and out came the other card players from their table.

"I can tell who the card shark in the family is." Jake's other half grinned at them. "It's sweet to see how well you guys work together. Not all men can grin so proudly when their woman beats them at anything. Especially cards."

"Oh, I'm not—" Mina started.

"No need to be modest." The brunette waved her off, taking a step forward. "You made up for beating the pants off of us every time Kent won. You'd grin at him like he hung the moon. Too cute." By now the others had gained a few steps on her. "It's good for Jake to lose once in a while. I'd better hurry or I'll never find them. Thanks for the fun game. And for the record, you guys make a lovely couple. You'll definitely go the distance."

"Oh, we're not—" Before Kent could utter the words *a couple*, the brunette had darted ahead and caught up with her friends out of earshot.

For a second, Kent didn't know what to say. Mina and her sister seemed to take the whole confusion in stride. One of the staff announced over the speakers that the rumba classes would begin in two minutes.

"We'd better hurry." Ginnie picked up her pace. "I want to hear how Jo's lessons went."

Following behind the two sisters, watching them laugh and revel in Mina's winning streak, he had to admit in their own way, they were two beautiful women. Both were friendly, smart, and pretty. Heck, he could say the same about Jo too, but it was Mina who in a short time had caught his interest. If he were honest with himself, more than caught his attention, she was beginning to work her way under his skin. Smiling came easy when he was with Mina and he liked that. A lot. Jim could make nice and party all night with all the single women he wanted. All Kent wanted was to learn more about what made this stoic woman tick, and he had less than a week to do so. Though, he had this odd feeling that he wouldn't mind taking a lot longer than that to uncover all there was to really know Mina Ummarino.

"We have an early tour tomorrow." Mina glanced at her watch. "We should probably call it a night."

Jo took a sip of her fruity drink. "I'm having a great time, but my feet are starting to feel it."

"Maybe," Ginnie pointed at her sister's spike heels, "if you wore more sensible shoes, your feet wouldn't hurt."

"True," Jo tipped her glass at her sister, "but I didn't get the height gene you two inherited."

With each Ummarino girl's birth, an inch or two were

shaved off their height. Mina was tallest at five foot seven. Ginnie came in next at five foot six and Jo came up the rear at only five foot four. Not that she was really short, but she had spent several teen years grumbling about the unfairness of being the only short one in the family.

"I'm old enough to know better and I still wear heels." Susan waved her hand at the three sisters and patted Jo on the arm. "There's something to be said for looking people in the eyes. You keep wearing your heels."

"Thank you."

Mina glanced around the large club. She'd caught herself more than once looking for any sign of Kent. She wondered if he was partying with Jim and the blonde, or if he had gone home early. Though that was highly unlikely, even if she did know that the two buddies had booked a tour of their own for early in the morning. He was a bit of an enigma to her, one that had caught her curiosity and wouldn't let go. A slow familiar tune played overhead and Mr. Findley reached for his wife's hand. "Shall we?"

The woman smiled sweetly and Mina wished she had someone to dance with too. Taking one more look around, she knew she wouldn't see Kent, but scanned the entire place anyhow. Pushing to her feet, she nodded at her sisters. "I'm calling it a night. Don't stay out late."

Jo nodded. "As soon as I finish this drink."

"And I," Ginnie grinned at her sister, "will keep you company."

Mina smiled and nodded at her next younger sister. "Good idea."

Sliding the card into the suite's door, Mina shoved it open, then stepping inside, kicked it closed behind her. Not wanting to trip and kill herself early in the trip, she flipped the light on and almost jumped out of her skin when Kent stood up from the couch.

"Sorry, didn't mean to startle you."

She tossed her card on the bar. "Why are you sitting here in the dark?"

He shrugged. "It's a lovely view."

Walking into the main living area, she glanced out the

open patio doors. He was right. The dark sea beyond shimmered under the moonlight. "It really is."

"There's a quiet out here that we don't get at home. It's nice."

Having inched her way onto the back deck, she nodded. "Yes. It is."

Grabbing the drink he'd set on the table, he walked within inches of her. "Penny for your thoughts?"

"Lots of things, I guess."

"Like?"

"Well, for one, I wonder how many breathtaking views are there in this world that I am clueless about."

"Considering it's a big world, I'm going to guess there's a lot. It's why people have bucket lists, I suppose."

Leaning against the railing, she turned to face him. "Do you have one?"

"A bucket list? Not really, but I'm thinking maybe I should put one together."

"Ditto."

He stood quietly at her side for a few moments before turning his back to the railing and facing her. "What were the other things you were thinking?"

"Honestly. If you promise not to laugh."

He drew an X across his chest.

"This suite is gorgeous but huge. Why the heck would a honeymoon couple need all this space?"

"You got me there. I can't imagine there are a lot of occasions for a honeymoon for five."

"What?" Her face twisted in confusion.

"Technically, there are five of us sharing this suite, so you might say it's a honeymoon for five."

"I don't know about that."

She shifted left at the same moment he shifted right and they wound up deep in each other's space. She could feel his warm breath against her face and knew she should step back, turn away, something to break the unexpected spell that seemed to pull them together like a pair of kitchen magnets.

She'd barely manage to gather her wits when Kent

cleared his throat and took a long step back. "We've got an early day. I'm going to call it a night."

"Yes." She nodded. "Me too."

He hesitated a minute and she wondered what else she should say, or do. Nothing came to mind. Nothing that made sense anyhow. The memory of the warmth of his hand on her back as they walked through the game room had her tempted to close the short gap he'd put between them, to find a reason for him to touch her again. A very dumb idea.

His gaze settled on hers and he smiled, almost as if he knew what she'd been thinking. "Sleep well."

"You too," she managed to softly respond.

Kent turned and not till he closed the bedroom door behind him did she turn and do the same. At least she knew one thing more that she hadn't known earlier. Kent Harwood was no party animal. And wasn't that nice to know.

CHAPTER SIX

"**W**hy would a cruise ship choose to dock at six o'clock in the morning when there are twenty three other hours in the day?" Mina stood in the middle of the room-size closet and grabbed her favorite deck shoes.

"Probably," Ginnie twirled her hair into a knot and stuck a clip in it, "because arriving at five would be even less well received."

"It's not the ship's fault we're running late." On the ground on all fours, Jo had her head under the bed searching for her shoes. "It's the dumb alarm's fault for not going off."

"It goes off just fine if you set it correctly." Ginnie slipped into her shoes.

Jo sprang up without her shoes. "I did set it right."

"We've got less than thirty minutes to get off this ship and catch the bus or miss our tour." Mina grabbed her room key. She'd have been just as happy to spend the morning in bed and the rest of the day on a relaxing desk side chair while her sisters combed the ancient island ruins. Not that she had anything against antiquities; she just wasn't fond of two hour bus rides that required getting out of bed before the chickens.

"How can I lose a pair of shoes in a single room? Suite or no suite, the place isn't *that* big." Jo stomped over to the closet Mina had just exited and put on what Mina had so often called her Pepto Bismol noisemakers. The kitten heel flip flops were cute but when Jo walked quickly the heels clicked on the floor and then the back of the shoe slapped against her foot. On a quiet day the noise could drive anyone nuts.

"Are you sure you want to walk ruins in those?" Even when Mina was the same age as Jo, she wore more sensible shoes. At least if there was a good deal of walking involved.

"They're very comfortable." Jo shrugged.

"Comfortable or not." Ginnie slipped her card into her neck pouch. "If we don't go now, and I mean now, the only place you'll be walking in those shoes is the promenade deck."

"What about breakfast." Jo looked at her watch. "Never mind. This is as good a day as any to try intermittent fasting."

Mina laughed. "Atta girl. Always finding the silver lining."

The three sisters laughed and hurried out the door and down the hall.

"Let's take the stairs. It will be faster than waiting for an empty elevator." Jo was already two steps down when Mina caught up to Ginnie staring at their kid sister.

Mina shrugged. "She has a point."

"Sometimes I hate it when the kid is right. At least we're not going up."

Hurrying to keep up with her sister practically skipping down the stairs, Mina had to chuckle. For a gal who was running on an empty stomach, her sister had enough energy for the three of them.

"Oh, good." Jo came to a stop at the bottom. "Another nice thing about being late is that the lines are short. Sort of like the airport. Everyone arrives early to stand on long lines so late comers check right in."

"Get your room cards out. The faster we clock out the sooner we can get off the boat." Ginnie already had her room card in hand.

Taking another step off the pristine carpeting onto the grated area leading to the gangway, Jo wobbled and then tipping to her right, stumbled upright, leaving a shoe behind. "Well, foo."

The kid held up one shocking pink sandal with a dangling heel.

"Maybe the town will have some sort of shoe store."

"Right." Jo rolled her eyes. "In the middle of an ancient archeological site, someone will have built a shopping center."

"Hey," Ginnie dropped her hands on her hips, "there's a Pizza Hut practically across the street from the Great Pyramids in Egypt. A shoe store isn't that unreasonable."

"Here." Mina slipped off her one shoe and handed it to her sister while she leaned the other way to remove the second shoe. "Wear these. I'll run upstairs and get another pair."

"There's no time." Jo frowned.

Mina looked at her watch. "Fifteen minutes. If I rush I can do it."

"What are you going to do?" Ginnie's fists remained on her hips. "Run *up* the stairs?"

The elevator nearby dinged and the door opened. Mina grinned at her sister, she loved it when timing came together. "Nope. Going against traffic now."

"Hurry." Jo called after her.

"Yes, ma'am. If I get hung up, don't wait for me."

"No," the two sisters echoed. "Just go."

"I'm going. But if the bus won't wait, you both go. I can find something else fun to do. Don't worry!" After all, she had been convincing herself she could be more adventurous.

The doors closed behind her and she kept a close eye on her watch. She was right about one thing. At this hour all the passengers were taking the elevators down to disembark, not going up. The elevator only stopped twice to pick up a few smart people who were going to the breakfast buffet instead of riding like sardines on a bus filled with tourists.

The elevator came to a stop on her deck and she bolted out before the doors were fully open. Almost running down the hall, she stuck her keycard in the slot just as the door swung open. "Oh." Her hand flew to her chest.

"Sorry." Kent stood in the doorway. "Didn't mean to startle you."

"I thought you and Jim had an early morning planned?"

"Jim and the blonde from the casino continued their winning streak after dinner. They had a very late night. He's still sleeping it off."

"Oh. Well. Hate to chat and run, but if I don't boogie, I'll miss the tour bus." She skirted past him, into the massive closet and holding a loafer in each hand, hurried barefoot past Kent. "See you later."

"Later," he repeated.

Busy looking at her watch, she debated the stairs or giving the elevator another shot when she almost took a tumble off the first step.

"Careful." Kent's fingers curled tightly around her right arm. "You'll ruin your vacation if you break your neck."

"Thanks." Steady on her feet again, she started down the steps two at a time. "Catch ya later."

Kent merely nodded, but he was following her down, doubling up on steps whenever she did. At the fourth floor, a family of nine million people had the same idea she had. A grandma and grandpa in no hurry to get downstairs and a young mom and dad maneuvering a stroller down the steps with a passel of additional young children, brought her to a screeching halt. Taking another quick look at her watch, she was only a little hopeful that the tour bus was as behind schedule as she was.

"Excuse us a second." Kent came up beside her and nudging her closer to the wall, maneuvered them past the teenage member of the family entourage, and then past the parents and their stroller. Grams and Gramps had already repositioned themselves in single file to allow others to move up or down more easily.

Successfully bypassing the slow moving family, still holding her shoes in her hands, she hurried down the last two decks only to be stopped again by a line twice the length of just a short while ago. "I'm never going to make it."

"What happened?"

She glanced at her watch. Her fifteen minutes were up. "Jo broke the heel of her shoe so I gave her mine and was hoping to get back before the tour left."

"I see." He nodded as they steadily moved forward. "What time is the bus leaving?"

Slipping one shoe on and then the other, she looked at her watch again. "Three minutes ago if they're punctual."

"Not likely." He smiled. "There's a reason people refer to island time. Sometimes I think the US is the only country on a time clock."

"From your mouth to God's ears." She reached the checkout podium, stuffed her card in, waited for the beep and before the crewman had time to nod, she was out the door and scurrying down the gangway. There were still a few busses at the end of the dock area. Hopefully one of them held her sisters. When she finally reached the buses, she glanced quickly at the signs each driver held high in the air. Shaking her head at the first sign, she hurried along the next parked bus, and another, before deciding the bus she wanted was most definitely not here. Apparently her driver was on a US time clock.

"They're gone?" Kent came up beside her.

"Looks like it."

"I know riding the back roads isn't the same as what you had planned, but I reserved two bikes for this morning if you'd like to join me."

"Bikes? As in motor or pedal?" And why was she asking that? If she was going to practice being more spontaneous, what difference did it make.

He laughed. "I'm afraid it's the old-fashioned human powered bicycle."

It had not only been years since she'd been on a bike, decades was probably more accurate. Maybe now wasn't the time to be adventurous. "I'm afraid I'd most likely hold you back. Especially if your plan involves pedaling up hill."

Smiling he shook his head. "That's the fun part of exploring on our own. No schedules. No itinerary. Just stopping wherever as long as we're back by four."

She let her gaze shift to the buildings in port and the little bit of the town visible beyond the gateway. Thick green colored hills rose up behind the small town. On a lovely day like today, casually taking a bike ride around the area actually sounded fun. A true adventure.

"If you get tired or bored we can turn back whenever you want," he coaxed.

Well, she'd been fussing that all the good food they were consuming practically twenty-four seven, and the pounds that came with it, was going to drive her to the gym when she got home anyway. No reason she couldn't start early with a little exercise disguised as fun and adventure. It was time for her to practice what she'd been preaching. "Sure. Thank you." Now she just had to hope that she didn't completely peter out after the first ten minutes.

From the look on her face, Kent wasn't sure which of them was more surprised that she'd said yes. "The bicycle rental office is supposedly just outside the port house."

"Sounds good. I'll just text my sisters. Their phones should be working now that we're on shore."

"I'm almost afraid to turn my phone on and see what's happening in the real world. When I first woke up I was tempted to turn it on and check messages and missed calls, but quickly decided whatever has waited this long can wait until after my ride."

"Not wanting anything to spoil the day." It wasn't really a question. Her gentle smile told him she understood how he felt. She finished her text and slid the phone in her shoulder bag. "Ready when you are."

Kent had forgotten the true meaning of island time. Even though today's tourists were all from the ships in port and needing to stick to schedules, the man in the single shack was in anything but a hurry.

"Do we have a plan?" Map in hand, Mina straddled the bright purple bicycle.

"There's an old church I'd like to see on the other side of the island. I'm not completely sure how bad the old road is. The ride might get a little bumpy, but the view is supposed to be one of the best on the island."

"Which means it's on the other side and up *that*." Her thumb pointed over her shoulder at the green hills behind her.

"It is." He shoved the kickstand up with his heel. "If you prefer, we could simply ride around the shore road."

Her grin lifted the corners of her mouth upward. "That's sweet, but not necessary. It's been a while, and if you promise not to laugh if I have to get off and push the bike up the mountain, we'll be fine."

"Fortunately for you, it's not a very big mountain."

"Height, like beauty, is in the eyes of the beholder. To me, at this hour of the morning, that thing might as well be the Rockies."

"For my sake I certainly hope not." He considered himself in pretty good shape, but biking up the Rockies would get the better of him.

"Lead the way." She waved him forward and then pushing the kickstand out of the way with her heel, took off beside him.

He did a quick u-turn. "I figure the sooner we get out of traffic the better, so I'm skipping the middle of town for now. Are you okay with that?"

Mina nodded. "Absolutely. I'm not thrilled about maneuvering past two ton cars or oblivious tourists."

"There's a little bar and grill on the must see island stops. It's right on the water and about thirty minutes outside of town. Does that work for you?"

"Anything that involves food is going to work for me. We skipped breakfast."

"Ditto." Neither said another word for the next thirty minutes. Only the wide grin on Mina's face showed him that she wasn't hating every minute of this. At least he hoped that's what the smile meant.

The sun shimmered on the calm sea waters. As they'd ridden along, the softest of waves would glide over rocks and sand. An occasional low rush of water would crash against the rocky shore, creating a splash and refreshing them with a sprinkle. He couldn't have ordered a nicer day for a bike ride.

"Isn't it a glorious day?"

"You won't get an argument from me."

The roar of an approaching engine broke the peaceful calm of the day. Kent veered to his right, waving Mina over. They'd shared the road with other cars passing by before, but this one sounded like he was confusing the island with the Monte Carlo Grand Prix. Sure enough, they'd barely eased over to the gravel side of the road when the car came zipping around the bend, and kicking up a breeze, blew past them, followed by another car almost climbing up his bumper.

"Idiots." Mina shook her head. "What the hell can be so important they have to travel at the speed of light."

"You said it yourself. Idiots."

She nodded and looked down the winding road the two cars had followed and pointed to a distant thatch roofed shack at the bottom of the road ahead. "Ooh. Tell me that's it."

"Only one way to find out if that's the Conch Shanty."

She chuckled. "I don't know about the name, but at this point I'm hungry enough to eat a whale." Her gaze met his and a wide cheeky grin took over her face. "Race ya."

He'd barely had time to process the words when she lifted up on the bike and took off like a jockey on a thoroughbred. Leaning forward, he gave it all he had and the two of them spit gravel as they practically flew down the road. Wind whipping in his face, he'd inched up on her and then she pulled out ahead of him once more. So the serious older sister had a streak of daredevil too. Who'd have thunk.

CHAPTER SEVEN

Streaking down the road, the sign for the Conch Shanty came into view several yards ahead of the quaint little hut. Veering away from the road, Mina followed the narrow drive and skidded to a halt in front of a small weather worn shack that painted the perfect image of the restaurant's name.

"Whew." She threw her arms into the air and lifted her face to the warm sun, then blew out a relaxed sigh. "I haven't done that since I was a kid."

He pushed the kick stand into place and climbed off the bike. "This is the second time you surprised me."

"How's that?"

"The first time was when you said you hadn't played cards since you were a kid and then proceeded to clean up. And now with the bike."

"So would that be that I can ride?" Unable to stop grinning, she stepped away from the bike. "Or that I beat you?"

"You only beat me because you took off without warning."

"Ha! You wish." If anyone had told her when she'd agreed to take this cruise that she'd be racing down a hill with a man she barely knew and loving every second of it, she would have had them committed. People like her simply didn't live on the wild side. Of course people like her rarely took real vacations either, so what did she know. She turned back to the parked bicycles. "Do you think it's okay to leave them here unattended?"

Glancing around, Kent frowned. "The guy at the rental shack said that most tourist spots had attendants who kept eyes out on the bicycles, but I don't see anyone. Do you?"

Hand spread over her brow, she looked from left to right. Opened her mouth to speak just as a young kid of about ten or twelve popped out from behind the building and flashed a toothy smile.

"I'll watch your bikes."

Kent nodded and smiling, waved at the kid before turning toward her. "Well, the guy never said how old the attendants would be."

She chuckled with him. "Entrepreneurs have to start somewhere."

In two long steps, he'd reached the entrance and held the door open for Mina. The minute they crossed the threshold, a variety of aromas smacked her in the face. All making her keenly aware of just how hungry she was.

"Oh man, this place smells good."

At his side, Mina raised her nose to the air sniffing out the delicious flavors. "I'll bet any amount of money I smell fried onions rings."

"Really?" He took another whiff. "Whatever is cooking smells delicious, but I couldn't begin to guess if it was fried onion rings or baked halibut."

"And I think I smell fresh bread too. Though it might be sweeter, like donuts." She shrugged. "What can I say? This Roman nose is good for something."

"If you're right, that nose of yours is amazing." His eyes instantly flew open, clearly suddenly concerned she might have taken offense at his impromptu comment.

His sudden rush of sensitivity was sweet, but she tipped her head back in a hearty laugh at his comment. "Thanks, but there are a lot of things my nose has been called, and amazing has never been one of them."

"Welcome to the Conch Shanty." A woman with very long dark hair pulled back in a ponytail, hugged a few menus to her chest with one hand, and waved at them to follow her with the other. The inside was much bigger than she'd expected from the exterior view. Pastel colored chairs surrounded small square wooden tables and spilled outside onto a large wooden deck. Admiring the gorgeous views from where she stood, it took a moment to realize there was no rear wall to the shack.

"Inside or on deck?" the woman asked.

Kent looked to her for input and she gestured with her chin toward the water. "On the deck, please. It's too beautiful a day to be inside, even if it does have a stunning view."

At the far corner of the open air seating section, they settled in at a two topper table with birds-eye views of all sides of the beach. The ocean water drifted within inches of the deck. Shifting her gaze from the ocean view to Kent holding his menu, but staring at her with buckled brows.

"This is none of my business, but your forehead is a bit rosy. Are you wearing sunscreen?"

Sunscreen. Her mouth fell open, and her eyes blinked slowly. She knew she'd forgotten something this morning. Any normal person would think the way the sun had been beating down on them, she would have remembered anywhere along the ride. "I forgot. I meant to bring a wide brimmed hat too, but in the rush to change shoes, I left it in the suite." Quickly, she reached for the small cross body purse she'd been wearing and had hung on the chair. "I have some in here I think."

She was almost positive she'd tossed the SPF 40 tube in her bag, but for a small bag it was deceivingly deep, finding the lotion took more effort than she'd expected. Finally wrapping her fingers around the tube and extricating it from her bag, she held it up triumphantly.

"There you go."

"This will only take a second." Squirting the sunscreen into her palm, she began slathering it on her face and hoped it wasn't too late.

"Don't forget your arms. We have a long day ahead of us."

She nodded. "Had I realized I was going to be spending most of the day out in the sun and not inside a bus, I wouldn't have worn a sleeveless top." She continued spreading lotion on her shoulders, arms, and the back of her neck before pushing her chair away from the table and leaning over to spread sunscreen on her feet. Once as a kid she'd neglected to use sunscreen on the tops of her feet and had to go barefoot for a week. While she was at it, she went ahead and slathered across the back of her calves and as far up the back of her thighs as she could reach without making a fool of herself in public. Satisfied she was sufficiently slathered, she waved the tube at him. "Need some?"

"No, thank you. I put some on before leaving the ship."

"Smart man."

He lifted his gaze from the menu. "I'm a morning person."

"So am I but it didn't seem to help me any this morning."

Their waitress appeared. "Are you ready to place your orders?"

"What do I smell cooking?" Mina asked.

The woman rolled her eyes playfully. "A lot, but what smells really good right now are the malasadas."

"The what?"

"The owner is from Hawaii. It's a Portuguese donut of sorts. They're delicious. I can recommend the fried onion rings and coconut shrimp."

"I knew that's what I smelled."

A few more minutes and their orders were placed, fresh mango drinks were served in a pineapple with colorful parasol in place, and the small appetizer sampler had her almost moaning with delight.

Kent stabbed at a popcorn shrimp. "The view is great and so far the food is delicious but it's much nicer with company."

"Thank you for the invitation. I love my sisters, but wasn't looking forward to the crowded bus ride."

"It might not have been that bad."

"No, not at all. Skinny seats designed for adolescents. Planned lunch at some truck stop that probably gives a kickback. Another stop at a discount shopping bonanza that most likely charges twice as much as anywhere not a discount outlet. Then sixty people following one man, or woman, waving an umbrella at us as we hover around unable to hear a word he or she is saying about the migration habits of some nearly extinct bird."

"Ooh. You paint a very vivid and unpleasant picture."

She chuckled. "Let's just say I'm willing to bet our lunch is going to be way better than anything my sisters have."

Lifting his pineapple in the air, he tipped his head. "To a delicious lunch."

"To a delicious lunch, and a relaxing afternoon." She tapped his pineapple with hers and decided that today was turning out okay after all. Better than okay.

If Kent thought he was going to have to take it easy, or a little more slowly, with Mina joining him for the day, boy had he been wrong. There had been moments on the narrow island road when even Jim would have been cautious with the occasional oncoming cars, and yet Mina would be coasting full speed ahead of him, arms in the air, and shouting silly things like "look Mom, no hands." He was pretty sure if her mother had actually been anywhere within view, the woman would have dropped on the spot with a heart attack.

To his surprise the oceanside road had not been the flat route he had expected, but rose up around the curves of the green lush hillside, and then back down again close to the shoreline. Every so often, up the hillside, there'd be a turn off for a lookout. They had stopped at almost every one of them. Some people might have gotten tired of the same ocean view, but not Mina. Each stop they'd sit on the rail, a tree stump, a large rock, or occasionally a bench that the tourism bureau might have provided. Anyone else, and he might've thought they were simply resting up for the next portion of the ride. Heaven knew he appreciated the occasional respite, but he could see a sense of appreciation in Mina's gaze that had little to do with aching muscles or sore derrieres.

"Do you get to the ocean often?" He hadn't wanted to breach the peaceful moment, but his curiosity had been growing with each lookout.

Her gaze fixed on some distant unknown point, she shook her head. "When we were kids our parents took us to Disney World. Before going home, my mom insisted that Dad make the hour long drive to the shore for a picnic on the beach. Having grown up in the landlocked Midwest, she hadn't been quite prepared for the sand getting into everything from the sandwiches, to constantly having the sand kicked onto the blanket, or ending up in our drink cups. Dad kept laughing and telling her things like, *that's why I suggested individual bottles so we could take a sip and screw the cap back on.* Or *that's why I suggested we put the sunscreen on before we hit the sand.*"

"How did Mom take that?"

"Considering every time he said something he'd lean over and kiss her on the cheek and add *I love you*, she'd simply laugh and responded *yes, dear.* But even though she was a little frustrated, she made sure that everybody still had a good time. I loved building the sandcastle, though I hated it when the water eventually crept up and washed some of it away. We collected seashells, buried my dad in the sand, jumped the waves, and had an all around memory making day."

"Is that what you think of when you're looking out at the ocean?"

She turned her head to look at him over her shoulder. "A little, yes. Mom always said she wanted to take another vacation on the beach, but we never got around to it. I may have to make more of an effort to not put things off so much."

"Things?"

"Fun things, like dinners out with friends, and shopping with my sisters, but especially taking a real vacation. Going places I've never been, seeing new things. It's too easy to put things off till another time, next year, when I have more money, when this project is done, etc. etc. etc."

He understood exactly what she was saying. Hadn't he

done the same thing? Focused on his career, his responsibilities, and the ordinary business of adulting, he'd said no to more invitations than he should have. "I understand the cruise line gives a discount if you sign up for another cruise while still on board."

"Really?" The serious expression on her face shifted into a contented smile.

"Yeah. I walked past the office where you can go in and sign up on my way back to the room yesterday."

"I may have to stop in and check it out." Her smile slipped. "Though I have no idea where or when I could go."

"From what I understand, that's the beauty of the whole thing. You don't have to commit to a particular cruise, you simply put $100 deposit down and get the early bird discount."

Her eyes widened and twinkled with delight. "I like that. No strenuous decision-making on the spot, but financial motivation to follow through." She bobbed her head, and still smiling, slapped her hands on her thighs and pushed to her feet. "What do you say we hit the road? We should be coming up on that church you want to see pretty soon."

Folding the large sheet of paper they'd been following all morning, he slid it in his back pocket. "According to this map, I'm pretty sure it's just around the next bend. We should come across a dirt road and follow it straight to the church."

Considering the church was off the beaten path, the map had been very easy to follow, and the road to the church was indeed just around the bend. To his surprise there was a small sign at the base of the road informing tourists of the church's existence. An even more pleasant surprise was discovering that the dirt road he had expected to find from his reading was actually a black top single lane road. Another pleasantry was discovering that rather than being the steep hill he had expected, the road actually wound around the hillside gradually bringing them to the top.

Unlike the shore road with ocean vistas, this road took them deep into the hills of the island. Surrounded by a canopy of tall trees and walls of tropical greenery, it was easy to forget they were even on an island.

"You holding up okay?" he called to her.

She didn't answer, only nodded.

This road was a bit steeper than any of the other hills they'd ridden. He had a feeling when they finally reached the church, sitting down would be a restful requirement. The greenery began to thin and at the top of the road a clearing appeared with a single building dead center.

"Oh, that is lovely." Mina came to a stop and still holding onto the handlebars, just took the old building in.

He dropped the kickstand and climbed off the bike. "The original church was built in 1685."

"Wow. I'm guessing this is not the original because it looks pretty good to be over three hundred years old."

"That's right. It burned to the ground in 1765 and was rebuilt in 1780."

She walked across the rubbled courtyard and stopped again. "Oh my, this is a magnificent view. Can you imagine having Sunday services and looking at that?"

"Makes you feel a little closer to God, doesn't it?"

"Hard not to." She whirled around. "Do you suppose it was Catholic?"

He nodded. "Most missionaries during the eighteenth century were Catholic. I'd say that's a safe guess."

"Then my mom would definitely love it. Do you think it's locked?"

"Only one way to find out." Together they followed the footpath to the front door.

Kent tugged at the door and was more than a little surprised to find it unlocked. "Well, how about this."

"I don't think I've ever been in anything this old." Walking slowly, she let her hand gently caress the dark mahogany benches. There were few windows and only the round window over the altar was done in stained glass. "I wonder if that has been restored through the years or if it has just survived a couple of centuries."

"I honestly don't know, but I do believe there's a curator of sorts who cares for it."

"I wish we could stay and watch the sunset from here. I bet it's beyond awesome."

"Speaking of sunsets." As much as he hated to bring it up, he had no choice. "It's getting late. We really should start back to the ship."

She nodded. "I'm afraid you're right. The witching hour is descending soon."

"Head back the way we came, or loop around the rest of the island?"

Her brows buckled, forming a deep line between her brows. "Which one is faster?"

"Six of one, half a dozen of the other."

"Then let's go all the way around."

"Works for me." A few minutes later, after one last glance out to sea, they were on their bikes and heading down the road so narrow it barely had room for the two of them side by side. "Don't take this one too fast."

"I may be occasionally daring, but I'm not stupid."

"Good to know." Something about this road made him a little too on edge. Once they reached the bottom, he blew out a relieved sigh. The rest of the ride would be smooth sailing. So to speak.

"I'll race you to the next lookout point."

And just like the time before, Mina was off and flying without giving him a chance to even think. Keeping up with this lady would be an interesting challenge for some man.

Coming around the next curve, the sound of roaring engines, much like he'd heard earlier in the day when the two racing drivers had whizzed past him, grew increasingly louder, closer. Here we go again. "Mina, let's move over." He wasn't sure if she'd be able to hear him, but was confident she had when she nodded, slowed her speed and veered right, hugging the edge of the road.

Just as they had before, the same two cars that had whizzed past them earlier in the day came zooming down the road. It didn't take much to recognize the two cars were bearing down on them and fast. Kent wasn't happy at all that these two were using the public road like a private Formula One racetrack. He could see the first car swaying in the road as the second car that seemed bound and determined to overcome the first car sleeked around him and then fell back again, not quite able to overtake the other car.

Kent mumbled words his mother would have washed his mouth out with soap over. Out in the middle of nowhere on a solitary road, there was nowhere for them to go and get out of these idiots' way. He'd called out to Mina, but she was too far ahead to hear. At least she seemed as aware of the speeding cars as he was. The two cars were quickly coming upon them and the hairs on the back of his neck prickled on edge. Sure enough, that second car once again made a move to overtake the first car and rather than give up his lead, the first car swayed slightly and veered in Mina's direction. There was no way she could keep her place on the narrow road. The car swerved away and then back in her direction one more time sending her bike, and her, off the road, over the rocky edge, and out of sight.

CHAPTER EIGHT

orror gripped at Kent's chest, nearly strangling the air from his lungs. He skidded to a stop and letting the bike fall to the ground, ran to where he'd lost sight of Mina. His heart still racing, he heard her before he saw her. Never had he ever thought that a moan would be a good sign. The ragged trail of rock between the road and the beach did not make for a soft landing. He didn't want to think of the damage the jagged stones could do.

Expecting to find the worst, his nerves settled at the site of Mina sitting upright on a large rock, shaking her head. First thing to cross his mind was thank heaven she was all right. The next thought was thank God they hadn't been on one of the higher spots on the road or the drop could have killed her. "Are you okay?"

"Define okay." She craned her neck toward the sun and blew out a long sigh. "I'm not sure I want to stand up."

"Why?" He climbed over the bigger rocks and past her mangled bicycle, once again thankful that she wasn't as bad as the bike, and crouched down beside her.

"I've got some good scrapes and scratches, but if I stand up, I might discover something more."

Close enough to get a good look at the scrapes and scratches she was referring to, he quickly scanned for any sign of inflammation. "Does anything in particular hurt?"

"You mean other than my pride?"

"Your pride?"

"I didn't see that car running *you* off the road."

"That's only because he didn't come close to me, but he got so up close and personal with you he could have kissed you before running you off the road."

"I could do without that kind of love." She shifted her weight, grimaced, and sighed. "And of course they didn't stop."

"Didn't even slow down." He reached for her ankle. "Speaking of personal, I want to just check your ankles."

"My what?" She continued to rub at the back of her neck.

"Before you get up, I just want to make sure we're not going to make matters worse."

"You a doctor and didn't tell us?"

He laughed. "Not even close. Boy Scout. Basic first aid."

Squinting from the sun, she pressed her lips tightly as if contemplating putting Humpty Dumpty back together again. "Fine."

With a brief nod, he gingerly lifted one foot, carefully watching her reaction. "Does this hurt at all?"

Lips still pressed tightly shut, she shook her head.

He dared to turn it a bit from side to side, and glanced up at her. He didn't have to say a word, she knew what he needed to know and shook her head. He did the same with the other foot and got the same response. "I'd say it could have been a lot worse. Ready to stand?"

"No, but I will." One deep breath later, she was on her feet and shifting from one foot to the other, tested her weight. "Looks like I'm no worse for wear."

"Too bad we can't say the same for your bike." The front wheel was completely folded in half, the rear wheel was flat, the chain had come loose, one of the pedals was nowhere to be seen and he was pretty sure there would be no straightening the handlebars any time soon. Considering the condition of the bicycle, he was truly amazed all she had were some scratches and minor cuts.

"And our ride back to town." Mina rolled her shoulders. "I have a feeling that I'm going to want to spend all of tomorrow's at sea day in the hot tub."

"Sore?"

She shook her head. "Just a little stiff."

Odds were she was more than stiff and just wasn't

voicing it. Yet. He pulled his phone from his pocket and turning it on, waited for the cell to come to life. The familiar carrier tune played and he waited for the bars. Nothing. Spinning about, he looked behind him and then out to sea. "No signal. How about you?"

Moving a little more slowly than usual, Mina slid her hand into her pocket and pulled out her own phone. One look at the screen and she shook her head as she tapped and pressed the power button. Her lips pursed together tightly, she stopped shaking her head and lifted her gaze to meet his. "I'm not going to be any help. I must have smashed it against the rocks on the way off the road."

"All right." He nodded. "If we want to make the ship, we'd better start walking back to the restaurant and call a cab."

"What about this thing?" She pointed to the mangled bicycle.

Smiling, he shrugged. "That's what insurance is for."

Slowly, she took a single step with the same caution a toddler learning to keep his balance might use.

"Need a hand?" Watching her gingerly move across the rocks, he could almost feel his mother jabbing him in the ribs to go help. Only years of dealing with modern independent women had him asking first.

"I got it. Thanks." Stepping off the last stone and onto the road, she stopped, and momentarily rubbed the back of her neck.

"Did you bump your head?" With the tumble she took on the rocky terrain, that was a very real probability, along with a concussion. That jabbing in his side from his mom just got harder.

"What?" She pulled her hand away from her neck and shook her head. "No, I'm fine." Moving her hand to shadow her eyes, she looked down the road in the direction of town. "Maybe I should wait here and you ride down to the restaurant."

He didn't need his mother poking him in the ribs to know there was no way he was leaving a woman alone on the road in the middle of nowhere, never mind one who may or may not have hit her head. Especially with a couple of crazy wanna be Formula One drivers on the loose. "If you're up to it, we'll both walk."

"Of course I'm up to it."

"Then shall we?" He bent at the waist and waved his arm with a flourish, garnering the smile he'd hoped for.

Side by side, they walked with Mina closest to the shore and his bicycle by the road. Just in case the lunatic drivers came back. And just in case, he kept a close eye on Mina as she walked, looking for any sign of a more serious injury. He wasn't sure if she'd hit her head or not, but the way she kept rubbing her neck, he suspected she had.

"I'm sorry I ruined your day, and broke the bike."

"For starters, you did not break the bike, those idiots did. And second, I should be apologizing to you for putting you in harm's way and now making you walk halfway to town."

"The exercise is probably good to keep me from getting stiff." She looked at him and smiled. "You know, you're being an awfully good sport about this."

"Not much I can do about it. Being a bad sport won't make things any better."

"Maybe bad sport was a poor choice of words. I forget not everyone is Italian."

"Excuse me?" Up until now he thought he was following the conversation just fine but he had no idea what being Italian had to do with being a bad sport or whatever she meant to say.

Mina chuckled. "You know, loud. Especially when something goes unexpectedly wrong. My parents are originally from New York. Combine loud and emotional Italians with loud spoken New Yorkers and, well, there's never a dull moment in the Ummarino household."

"Big family?"

"Very. There are three of us, and we're the smallest. My mom and dad each have four siblings and almost everyone has at least four kids. Though we do have a couple of aunts and uncles who are still in New York. My dad's parents died when we were kids but my Grandma Le is still around and lives with Mom and Dad."

"Oh, that must be nice."

"It has its pros and cons. Most days my mother is delighted to still have her mother around. Some days Mom will be marching through the house muttering *If it ain't one thing, it's your mother.*"

That made Kent laugh. "I think I'd like your mother."

Mina's smile widened. "Everyone does. Especially if she's cooking. There isn't a friend or foe who wouldn't kill for Mom's lasagna."

"Now I know I like her."

"Oh, look. We were closer to the restaurant than I thought." Mina pointed ahead and winced.

"What's wrong?"

"Nothing." She shook her head.

He was pretty sure nothing was something, but he wasn't going to push it. Yet. A couple more minutes and they reached the Conch Shanty. Only the doors were locked. "Wait here."

Trotting around the building, he hoped to find staff around back. The only thing he discovered was that the open view wall was now sealed with roll down glass doors. Now what?

Unfortunately, Mina hadn't paid much attention to the sign on the door when they'd come to eat earlier.

"There's no one around back." Kent trotted up to where she stood. "I guess they close down between lunch and dinner."

"Not exactly."

"What do you mean?"

She pointed to the sign with the arm that wasn't hurting. "They only open when a ship is in port."

"But we are in port."

"Yes, but the ship leaves at five. All aboard is four. So no point in staying open now."

He sighed as understanding dawned. "No dinner guests."

"Apparently this isn't a local's hangout."

Once again he tried his phone.

"I gather from that frown still no signal?"

"No signal." He stuffed the phone back in his shirt pocket. "As much as I hate to say it, looks like we're walking back and hopefully someone will come by to give us a ride the rest of the way."

Since the only cars they'd seen since coming down from the hilltop view were the two idiots who had run them off the road, she wasn't holding her breath on this one. She just wished their phones worked.

"Are you feeling okay?"

"Fine, thank you." There was no point in mentioning that the pain in her wrist had begun to radiate up her arm.

"Then why are you frowning?"

"Am I?"

He nodded.

"I guess I was thinking about what happens if we miss the ship. My sisters are going to be worried as all get out."

"There's still hope that somebody will drive by. After all, this is not exactly a deserted island."

"No, but if our little restaurant is any example, we do seem to be on the lesser inhabited side of the island. Not to mention, more than a short walking distance to the boat."

Now Kent was the one frowning. "I certainly wouldn't mind letting all the air out of those two idiots' tires."

"I was thinking something more appropriate like throwing their car keys into the ocean might make me feel better." Though right now she'd settle for a couple of ibuprofen to stop the throbbing in her elbow.

"I might find that satisfying if we could throw the car in along with the keys."

A cross between a snort and a chuckle escaped her lips.

"You should do that more often." Kent smiled at her.

"What, snort like a pig with a cold?"

His grin broadened. "Laugh."

Her baby sister was one to tell her that often. Of course

with each added child, the rules of the Ummarino family had become more lax so that the baby of the family had grown up more spoiled then she or Ginnie had. Thankfully, she grew up into a nice person and a friend who took life a bit less seriously then Mina did.

"You're frowning. Thinking of your sisters again?"

She nodded. "Jo was such a spoiled little thing. We're the typical family. First born has all the rules and regulations. No dating till sixteen. No makeup till high school, and even then with great reluctance. No cell phones, tablets, and restricted TV time. With Ginnie, most of the rules still applied with a few perks, but by the time Jo came around no one cared how much TV she watched, if she played computers and the first time she whined that all her friends had cell phones, she got one too."

"What about dating and makeup?"

"The makeup was junior high. Dating, she wasn't in near as much of a hurry. Not that with her northern Italian blonde hair and blue eyes she didn't have plenty of boys practically drooling over her. But, despite it all, she turned out pretty good. She's got a sharp mind and good heart."

"And you love her very much."

Despite the increasing pain in her arm, she smiled hard. "Yep. Would die for either of my sisters."

"I don't have any sisters, but I would walk through hell and back for my brother."

So many siblings didn't care about each other. She never understood that. "Speaking of walking, how long do you think it's going to take to reach town?"

Now he was the one frowning. "I'm not sure."

"But you're worried we're going to miss the boat too?"

"Not worried, just thinking through the possibilities."

"What I don't get, is why are so few people on this side of the island?"

"No clue, but it's awfully pretty this way."

"I know. Everything is so built up back home and getting more and more crowded. All this back to nature makes a person think."

He nodded and looked to his watch.

"How long have we been walking?"

"Too long. The ship should be leaving port in another half hour."

Her gaze drifted down the road to a large swath of land that jetted out between the road and the shore. "Funny how this road twists and turns into and away from the shore."

"Reminds me of some old cities where the streets were paved along old cow trails. Those roads go in the strangest directions."

"Look." She lifted her bad arm to point and winced, immediately pressing it against her chest and using her other hand to point ahead.

"Hey." Kent stopped short and spun around to face her, his gaze focusing on the arm now held tightly against her. "Blast."

CHAPTER NINE

How had Kent not noticed before that Mina was hurt? He should have paid more attention. "I'm going to take a closer look at your arm."

"Not necessary. It's just bruised from the fall, probably sprained."

"I don't think so. Your wrist is only slightly swollen but that elbow is the size of a grapefruit. Can you move your fingers?"

"Honestly, I don't have a clue. Not too sure I want to know." Sporting a forced smile, clearly gathering her gumption, she wiggled her fingers and sucked in a sharp breath. "Yes, I can move them, but I'd rather not do that again."

"Please let me check out the arm. I promise to be careful."

"If you hurt me, I promise to hurt you more." The sneer designed as a smile told him that her comment was no idle threat.

As gently as he could, he pressed along her fingers and palm. "Can you feel this?"

She nodded.

"Does it hurt?"

"Not really."

"Not really?"

"Let's say touching my hand doesn't make my arm hurt any more."

He carefully pressed at her wrist. "I think you're probably right about the sprain with your wrist." His fingers followed the length of her forearm and with as much care as he could, he tried to move her arm to get a better look at the elbow, until she gritted her teeth and squeezed her eyes shut. "You probably landed on your wrist and jammed your elbow. This isn't swelling from inflammation, it's blood."

"Well, whatever it is, it hurts like a son of a bee if I move it or my fingers."

"I bet." He grabbed the edge of his shirt and lifted it over his head.

"What are you doing? You'll fry without your shirt."

"You need a sling. Besides, don't you still have sunscreen left?"

"I do, but I am not wearing your shirt. I can hold it like this just fine."

He was going to have to add stubborn to that protective streak she had. Ignoring her protests, he tied the corners together. "I don't need a shirt but you, on the other hand, need help holding that arm."

"I really don't—"

"No arguments." He held it up high near her head. "Please." For a few tense seconds he thought she was going to continue to protest until she blew out a deep sigh and dipped her head so he could slide the make-shift sling over.

"I'll wear it, but only because of that house."

"House?" He carefully helped her ease her hand into the makeshift sling before looking up. "What house?'

"The one I was going to show you when you noticed my arm."

Following the direction her left arm was pointing, he spotted a structure completely hidden by trees and plants, what looked like the roof of a small building peeked out at them. "Fingers crossed that whoever they are, they have a car and can get us to the ship on time."

"We'd better boogie." Without waiting for him, she took off walking at a near trot.

"Don't you ever give a person a heads up?" He was teasing, but this taking off before he could even process her words was becoming a pattern.

At the quick clip they both walked, it didn't take long to reach the dirt cut off from the road that seemed to lead to the house that already was slightly more visible. By the time they reached the walkway to the front door, it was clear the house was bigger than it looked from the road.

Mina slowed her pace and glanced around her, almost mesmerized by the lush landscape. "There are days when living someplace like this, away from people and chaos, surrounded by oxygen producing plants holds a great deal of appeal."

"That it does." The house and landscape wasn't the only thing that held a great deal of appeal. All day he'd been trying to ignore the smile that lit up her eyes, the laugh that came from deep in her heart. Outdoors, without makeup, with chestnut hair pulled back in a ponytail, Mina was still the most beautiful thing he'd seen on the island all day. Pushing his thoughts far away, he stepped onto the front stoop and not finding a doorbell, knocked.

"Doesn't look like anyone's home." Mina sighed heavily. The way she mindlessly used her good hand to rub her sore upper arm, he was pretty sure it was hurting more than before.

"Give me a minute, let me see if maybe someone is around back."

Mina nodded.

The house was simple and the exterior well kept. That said a lot about the occupants. As he turned the corner from the ample side yard into the back, he spotted a woman leaning over a massive vegetable garden. "Hello." She didn't move so he moved closer and called again. When he got closer, he could hear the music playing and called out one more time, "Excuse me. Hello."

The woman sprang back and landed on her bum.

"I'm sorry, I didn't mean to startle you." He extended his hand to help her to her feet.

Chuckling softly, she shook her head and pulled her gloves off. "My fault. I didn't hear you coming. We don't get many visitors out here."

He could certainly understand why. "I'm sorry to bother you, but I was hoping you might have a car and could give us a ride back to the ship?"

"*Touristas.*" She smiled, then turned her wrist and

frowned. "You come on one of the cruise ships?"

"Yes. We did."

"We?" She looked over his shoulder and frowned again. "*Donde esta*? Where is the other person?"

"In front. We knocked at the door, but there was no answer. We're hoping you can give us a ride to port?"

Shaking her head, she tossed her gloves into the basket at her feet and began walking toward the front of the house. "Yes, we have a car, but it's at the *taller*, the mechanic's. My husband took it this morning, but it wouldn't do you any good even if we did. The ship should be leaving any minute."

Looking at his own watch, he thought they still had almost an hour, and if the ship was running even five minutes late, that would give them even more time to make it back to port. Enough time *if* they had a car.

"You forget the time?" She pointed at his wrist.

Smacking his open palm across his forehead, he nodded. The captain had announced in the morning not to forget that the ship was departing on island time, not ship time, and that the island was one hour ahead. "Yes, I'm afraid so."

As she turned the corner by the front entrance, her steps slowed and her eyes opened wide. "*Mija*. What happened?" The woman hurried to where Mina stood.

"We had a little accident."

The woman looked at the makeshift sling and then back at Kent, or more specifically, his bare chest. Then she noticed the bicycle leaning against the house. "Only one bicycle?"

Mina nodded. "Yes. I'm afraid mine is on a hillside a ways back."

"Come inside. You must be tired and thirsty."

"We'd like to try and make it back to the ship." Especially if the ship was less than punctual. "Can we use your phone? Maybe call a cab." Kent followed the woman inside.

The woman shook her head. "I am sorry, but the phone lines came down two hurricanes ago and have yet to be repaired."

Unless a miracle was on the horizon, it was time to admit that he and Mina were not going to reach the ship on time.

Right about now Mina would kill for a couple of aspirin. Her sisters must be beside themselves with worry. They needed to get back to town and get word to them.

"Sit. My husband is in his workshop. He should be here soon and then we'll have dinner."

Mina shot a glance in Kent's direction at the same time he turned to look at her. She wanted to get back to town, contact her sisters, and figure out how to rejoin the cruise. Staying for dinner with the locals was not on her agenda.

"We really would like to get to town. Mina should see a doctor for her arm." Kent had said what she was thinking.

"I'm afraid you're going to have to wait till morning to return to town."

"Morning?" Mina hadn't meant for that to come out so squeaky.

Their hostess nodded and shrugged at the same time. "It is not safe for you to walk or ride your bicycle after dark, and the sun will be setting soon. You stay here. Go to town in the morning."

It suddenly occurred to Mina that this nice older woman and her husband might not be as innocent as they appeared. She wasn't a pessimist by nature, but she didn't want to wind up on the six o'clock news as the couple that went on a ride into the island hillside and then disappeared.

"In the meantime, I get some ice for that arm." The woman walked away and Mina chastised herself for thinking their hostess was anything more or less than what she appeared to be. A nice lady doing her best to make them feel at home in her house.

An ice pack wrapped loosely around her elbow, Mina had almost dozed off on the sofa when their host came through the back door. A surprisingly tall man compared to the other locals she'd seen in town before they'd ventured off on their adventure, he stopped short in his tracks at the sight of Mina and Kent on his sofa.

Before the beefy man could say a word, his wife came scurrying into the small living area, wiping her hands on the edge of her apron and grinning at her husband. "We have company for dinner."

The husband's gaze narrowed when it landed on Mina's arm and then Kent's shirtless state.

"They had a little accident. Missed their ship." She gave him a slight peck on the lips. "Wash up, and get a shirt for Mr. Harwood."

"Kent, please," Kent interrupted.

"And call me Mina."

"I'm Ramon Garza." The man extended a hand to Kent. The look of concern that had lingered in his gaze seemed to take a backseat to hospitality. "Welcome. You're in for a treat. Cecilia is one of the best cooks on the island."

"One of?" his wife teased him.

Ramon chuckled and kissed his wife on the tip of her nose. "You and I both know you are the best, but it's better to at least appear humble."

"Good point." His wife nodded, grinning. "Supper is ready."

The house was bright, airy, and simple in its décor. The rooms were neither large nor small and the same could be said about the eating area Cecilia had led them to. A few minutes later and Mina was diving into the most delicious dish of rice and beans she'd ever had. Who knew ordinary white rice could taste this good.

"I made the *carne mechada*, shredded beef, so you don't need two hands and a knife."

"This is totally delicious." Mina dug in for another forkful.

"Reminds me of *Ropa Vieja*." Kent dangled his fork in the air ready for another bite. "My neighbor growing up was Cuban and made dishes similar to this that tasted almost as good."

"Yes," Cecilia nodded proudly, "my grandparents were originally from Cuba."

"How is that arm feeling?" Ramon asked.

Not until the food was placed in front of her had she realized how hungry she was. She'd been enjoying the meal so much that she'd almost forgotten about her arm. "Tolerable."

"Now that you have food in your stomach, we should give you something for the pain." Cecilia pushed away from the table and returned with a bottle of much appreciated ibuprofen. "This will help you feel better. Tomorrow morning when the mechanics bring our car back, Ramon will take you into town. You can see a doctor then."

Mina nodded. They didn't really have any choice. Not about the doctor, but waiting till morning to head into town. Dinner had been delicious, and despite the pain in her arm, the company and conversation had been more pleasant than she could have expected. Cecilia and her husband had retired to the quiet side of the island a few years ago. He enjoyed making hand carved souvenirs and furniture, Cecilia was perfectly content growing her own vegetables and painting sea shells. After dinner they'd taken a tour of the workshop.

"These are amazing." Holding a small piece of what was once simple driftwood and was now a smooth shiny statue of a pair of dolphins at play. Another piece a bird in flight. And still another an owl perched on a much larger branch. The pieces were small and lifelike and others large and abstract. All of them absolutely stunning. "I can't get over how beautiful they all are."

"How long have you been working with driftwood?" Kent stood staring at a small abstract on a small stone base.

Ramon crossed the room to stand beside him. "I have tinkered with these since childhood. My grandfather gave me my first carving knife. He was a master whittler. The hard part is finding the pieces that speak to me."

"These certainly speak." Mina shifted to the other side of the workshop to where Cecilia's paints and easels were set up. A half shell the size of her palm with a sunset seascape painted to excruciating detail caught her eye. Afraid to touch, she leaned in for a closer look. The miniature painting was almost mesmerizing in its simple beauty. "So much talent in one family."

"You like?" Cecilia came to stand next to her.

"It's beautiful."

Smiling, Cecilia picked the shell up and placed it in her hand. "You keep."

"Oh, I couldn't." She had no idea how long these took her to make, but surely this was their livelihood.

Still smiling, Cecilia squeezed Mina's good arm. "I insist. It makes me happy to have my work with someone who appreciates it so much."

"Thank you. I will treasure it always."

"Good." Cecilia clapped her hands together. "Now it's late. We'll get you settled in for the night."

The pathway from the workshop to the house was narrow, and slightly uphill, but only took a few minutes to reach the quaint family home. At the back door, Mina turned to look down the hillside. The beach was a long walk away. "It's so quiet."

Kent stopped beside and followed her gaze. "Quite a contrast to city living."

All she could do was nod. No phones, no cars, no central heat and air, but plenty of peace, quiet, fragrant flowers, and happy people. Made her rethink the American dream of streets lined with gold.

"Yeah." Kent nodded.

She turned to face him. "Yeah what?"

He smiled at her. "Makes you think."

"Yeah. It does." Following her hosts inside, she cast a quick glance at Kent. Was she so easily readable by a near stranger that he knew what she was thinking about or was contemplating the pros and cons of the modern world a normal expectation under the circumstances?

"Here you go." Cecilia opened a door at the end of the hall.

"It's very kind of you to put us up for the night," Kent spoke what Mina had been thinking. Maybe they did think alike.

"Nonsense. It has been lovely having new people to visit with." Cecilia walked over to the window and pulled the lightweight curtains closed.

"Here you go." Ramon came in the doorway, a stack of folded clothes in his hands. "My wife thought a button-down shirt would be easier for the Mrs. with that banged up wing."

Mrs?

"The mechanic won't have the car back until mid morning so feel free to sleep in. You already know where the bathroom is. Up the hall, first door to your right." Cecilia was already standing at the door again, her hand on the knob. "Sleep well."

The door eased shut with a click and Mina slowly glanced from the door to the bed and then to Kent. *Oh boy.*

CHAPTER TEN

Oh boy. Kent glanced at the bed. A king size would have been easier to deal with, especially since he could feel the panic building in Mina at their unexpected sleeping arrangements. He wasn't all that calm about it either. He couldn't even do the typical rom-com hack of sleeping in the tub. At least not with the only tub in the house being down the hall.

Still staring at the clothing Ramon had handed her, Mina wasn't moving.

The room was small by some people's standards, with limited furnishings. The bed along one wall, a small table at each side, mismatched lamps on the two night tables, and a small dresser and mirror were the only items in the bedroom. No chair for him to sleep in and he'd already established no tub. Thanks to the warm tropical weather, the bedding didn't include anything like a thick comforter to substitute for a mattress on the floor. Though now that he thought about it, there wasn't much room on the floor for him either, but comforter or no comforter, space or no space, the floor was his only chivalrous option. "I'll take the floor."

Mina finally looked up. "You can't do that."

"Can't?"

"You know what I mean."

"Well, I can't sleep in the bathtub."

She shook her head and sighed. "That wouldn't be any more comfortable than the floor anyway. I never understood why the movies make that a suitable option."

That made him laugh. There were a lot of things that struck him as ridiculous in movies. "Like the victim going alone into the dark dangerous basement."

"Exactly."

Taking another look around the room he rubbed the back of his neck. "Okay. Next best scenario."

"I'm listening."

"You get in bed under the sheet and I'll sleep on my side on top of the sheet. It won't be the wall of Jericho but it will have to do."

Mina chuckled. *"It Happened One Night."*

"Very good. Most people wouldn't have made the connection."

"Most people weren't raised by an old movie buff."

"Then we agree?"

She nodded, handing him a large t-shirt that she assumed was for him. "Agreed."

In light of the fact that he hasn't worn a shirt for hours, it seemed almost silly in this heat to bother. On the other hand, under the uncomfortable situation of sharing a bed in a non-romantic fashion with someone of the opposite sex, a shirt might not be a bad idea. "Thank you."

"I don't want to hurt her feelings, but I really don't want to try and squirm out of the top I'm wearing."

"How's the arm doing?"

A knock sounded at the door. Since Mina was closest, she opened it.

Cecilia stood on the other side with a glass of water in one hand, shaking a pill bottle with the other. "You'll need these for that arm."

"Thank you." Mina bit back a smile and closed the door. "Considering how often she made me ice my elbow throughout the evening, I shouldn't be surprised she's still fussing over me. Makes me feel like I'm home with Mom."

"I gather from your smile that's a good thing."

"Very." Mina walked over to the bed and pulled back the covers. "Mom may drive me nuts from time to time, but I can't imagine having anyone else for my mother."

Kent waited for her to settle in before sitting down himself on the bed. "Hovering seems to be a genetic quality in most mothers."

"Do you get along well with yours?"

"For the most part, yes. Other than when she nags me to find a nice girl and settle down, we get along really well. I'm hopeful that Shane and Melody will have a baby soon and take the heat off of me."

"Who is older, you or Shane?"

"I am."

"Any more siblings?"

He shook his head. "We come from a long line of small families."

"I can't even imagine. If Mom hadn't run into complications when Jo was born so she couldn't have any more, she probably would have probably had at least a half a dozen of us. Italian, you know."

"Right. Big families."

"If having thirty-eight first cousins means big, yes."

"Thirty-eight?" Kent knew his jaw had dropped open but snapping it shut took an extra second. "Quite the contrast to our long line of small families. Mom has a sister. Dad's an only child."

"Must make for quiet holiday gatherings."

"I guess." He had friends with larger families, but he rarely gave much thought to what their holidays were like compared to his.

Leaning back against the headboard, Mina stared up at the spinning ceiling fan.

"Penny for your thoughts."

"My sisters are going to kill me."

Kent chuckled to himself. "Jim might not even notice I'm gone."

"I don't believe that for a minute."

"Okay. He'll notice, but I doubt he'll worry. Maybe he'll help your sisters keep calm about the whole thing."

"Maybe." She leaned to her right slightly and winced.

"How bad is it?"

"Actually, if I don't move it doesn't hurt very much at all. But it doesn't take much to remind me I'm injured." Shifting, she raised her left arm across herself and flipped the lamp switch, collapsing heavily back in place.

Had he been thinking, he would have suggested she take the other side of the bed. If only there was something he could do to make her feel better. If he could, he would take away all her worries and discomfort. There was a lot to Mina, and the more he got to know her, the more he liked her. Probably a lot more than he should. Turning, he pulled the chain on his lamp, sending the room into darkness. "Good night."

"Good night."

Now all he had to do was ignore the fact that he had a beautiful woman at his side. A very special beautiful woman. Closing his eyes and remembering how he felt watching her fly off the road, he accepted sleep was not going to be his friend. Tonight was undoubtedly going to be a very long night.

The ceiling fan was already spinning at full speed. Despite the breeze, the room was still uncomfortably warm. Of course Mina knew it had little to do with the tropical climate and everything to do with the man lying at her side. At least he was wearing a shirt now. She'd almost swallowed her tongue when he'd pulled it off to make a sling. The guy either worked out or lied about a desk job. Broad shoulders, strong muscles, and washboard abs you could scrub a tub of laundry on hadn't been easy to ignore.

She had no idea how much time had passed since they'd turned out the lights, but she was sure this might prove to be the longest sleepless night of her life.

"Arm bothering you?" The deep, low, almost sleepy voice, smoothed over her like a warm comfy quilt.

"I'm sorry. Am I keeping you awake?"

He was silent so long, she thought he wasn't going to answer. "My mind wants to jump ahead to tomorrow instead of catching forty winks."

"The quiet isn't helping."

Kent chuckled. "Like *I Love Lucy*. When they moved to

the country. We need some squirrels to play on the roof.”

"Or *My Cousin Vinny*. A small riot would do.”

"I love that movie. Never gets old.” Kent punched at the pillow behind him and sat up. “Always thought it was a shame Fred Gwynne died so soon after that movie. It was the first time I’d seen him and completely forgotten about Herman Munster.”

"What’s a yewt?” She couldn’t help but chuckle. Pushing on her good arm, she slowly eased upright as well.

"Here.” Kent grabbed one of the pillows and propped it behind her. “Better?”

She nodded. “Yes. Thank you.”

"What’s your favorite part?”

"Of what?” Because there was no way she was going to say the gentle way his fingers held her arm as he stuffed the extra pillow behind her was easily a favorite part of the day.

"*My Cousin Vinny*.”

She laughed. “Oh, that’s easy. The biological clock scene. Not just the way she goes on, but the way she comes back with maybe this wasn’t the best time to bring it up. What’s yours?”

"When Joe Pesci sits back, crosses his arms and ankles, and tells his cousin to *watch this* while Marissa Tomei’s character testified about the car.”

"Oh, yes. I love that one too. Or when Vinny asks the witness and *only* the witness to count fingers.”

"There were a lot of funny scenes and no matter how many times I see it, they never get old.”

"I know. I have favorite movies I could watch over a thousand times and still find them fun.”

"What’s you’re all time favorite?’

"That’s hard. I suppose if I could only watch one movie it might be *Apollo 13*. Who doesn’t love a true story happy ending?”

"Agreed. Pretty much everything Ron Howard touches is golden.”

"True, but usually I’m more partial to movies made long before Ron Howard.”

"Like?”

"I like the odd ducks. Movies that most people have never heard of are some of my favorites."

"Like?"

"Well. I guess one of my favorite comedies is *Buona Sera, Mrs. Campbell.*"

"With Gina Lolabrigita."

She bit back the pain that shot up her arm when she turned too quickly to face him. "You've seen it?"

"Don't look so surprised. It's a funny movie."

"I thought I was the only one who watched movies made before even my mother was born."

He shook his head. "My mom always had old movies on. When we were little kids we weren't allowed to watch a lot of television, but Mom always had the classic movie channels on while she worked around the house, or on some project. Sometimes the movies would be on and she wasn't even in the room."

"So now you and your brother are old movie buffs?"

"Nope. Shane wasn't big on sitting still. The only TV he wanted to see had to involve sports or racing."

"Funny how siblings can be raised in the same house, by the same parents, and turnout completely different."

He nodded his head "Talking about you and your sisters?"

"Yes and no. We are very different, but I've got friends who are identical twins and are nothing alike."

"Mother Nature is very complex."

"Definitely." The conversation fell into silence and the need to fill the emptiness with words wasn't there. Maybe it was because she was finally fading or maybe it was just that comfortable silence that she was always reading about.

"I suppose we should try again to get some sleep." He turned and pulled the switch on his light.

"I have a feeling tomorrow's going to be a long day." More carefully than when she had pulled up on the bed, she scooted back down under the sheet. "If my sisters hand me my head on a silver platter, promise me you'll tell my mom and dad I love them."

Kent chuckled again. She tried not to laugh with him,

the movement jarred her elbow more than she wanted it to, but she liked how easy it was to laugh with him. Too easy. For the next couple of hours, they continued chatting about everything from food, to art, back to movies, then travel, bucket lists, and just about everything under the moon and sun. At some point Kent reminded her it was time for her pills. The concern in his eyes made her heart do a little flip. She wasn't sure when she'd fallen asleep, but she'd slept soundly on a cloud. Not even the discomfort in her arm had disturbed her.

Somewhere in her dreams, she'd snuggled into the comfy bed only to realize now that the sun was peeking through the closed curtains, that bad arm and all, what she'd snuggled into was Kent.

CHAPTER ELEVEN

The sheets kicked away, Kent had spent the last hour watching Mina sleep. On her left side, her right leg thrown over his, her head tucked against his shoulder, her hair tickling his nose, and her right hand gently resting on his chest. She hadn't moved an inch in all that time and he didn't dare move and jar her injured arm. One of the things that had caught him off guard in the last twenty-four hours was the overwhelming need to protect her. Slow and easy, he brushed the edges of her hair away from his nose and enraptured by the soft feel, gingerly finger combed the silken strands.

He knew the second she woke up. Her slow and steady breathing almost stopped. He could feel the tension ricochet across every inch of her. "Good morning."

It took her a few seconds to respond, sucking in a wince, pushing away from him, she managed to sit upright. "Morning."

A knock sounded at the bedroom door. "Breakfast is ready."

"Thank you!" Mina called. "We'll be right there."

"If I didn't think she was enjoying having more people to fuss over, I'd feel guilty making her work so much." Kent wished they could have a few more minutes alone, but there was no point in playing with fire.

Throwing his feet over the side of the bed, he considered their situation. "I think it best if the car isn't back by the time we're done with breakfast, I should ride into town and send word to the ship."

Lips pressed tightly together, Mina stared so intently he was convinced she was reading his mind. Her shoulders relaxing, she nodded. "As much as I hate waiting behind, you're right."

Kent pushed to his feet. "I'll flip you for who gets to brush their teeth first?"

"I'd fight you for that, but we don't have any toiletries."

"Care to lay odds on whether or not Cecilia already thought about that?"

She failed to bite back a chuckle. "You're probably right. You go first."

Teeth brushed with the two new brushes and single tube of toothpaste that Cecilia had placed in the bathroom, they made their way to the kitchen. Their hostess had also seen to it that they had fresh towels and two clean shirts. A t-shirt for Kent and another button down for Mina. Now the small table was covered with delicious smelling food that had Kent's stomach churning with a different kind of hunger.

"There you are." Frying pan in hand, Cecilia scooped up toasted rounds and set them on a plate already piled high with more of the pancake-looking treats. "I hope you like coconut fritters."

"Ooh, sounds delicious." Mina glanced around the food covered table. "You've been busy."

Cecilia grinned at her. "I wasn't sure what you'd like. I considered French toast and then decided coconut fritters might be something special for you. Of course, you need protein. How do you like your eggs?"

"Whatever is easiest." Kent reached for a warm fritter. Cecilia had been right about that. Despite all his travels, he'd never had one before. And, of course, they did not disappoint.

"You like?" Cecilia glanced up from the bowl of eggs she was beating.

"Like? They're delicious."

"Good. Enjoy. In the meantime, my Ramon borrowed your bicycle and rode into town early this morning. He's going to notify the cruise line that you're okay. As soon as the car is ready, he'll be back to take you to town."

"That was very kind of him." Mina dug into the scrambled eggs that Cecilia had slid onto her plate.

Cecilia nodded. "How's that arm feeling?"

"The same."

"Hmm." Cecilia frowned. "I was hoping it would be better with a night's rest. Ramon is also going to reach out to Dr. Vega."

"Any idea how long he'll be?"

Cecilia shook her head. "Not long I expect."

True to her word, as they were finishing up the morning feast, Ramon came through the front door, another man behind him.

"Car isn't ready so I hitched a ride with Dr. Vega."

"House calls?" Kent didn't mean to say that out loud.

The doctor smiled and set his bag down on the table. "Many things about island life are different from the United States. As fate would have it, I was free to bring Ramon home. He tells me you have a banged up arm."

Mina nodded. "It's my elbow that hurts."

"I see. Let's have a look."

Kent had expected them to go to a different room; instead, the doctor helped her slip out of the makeshift sling and slowly lifted her arm. Each time Mina grimaced, Kent had to bite back the urge to knock the doctor out of the way and tell him to leave her alone. He was reacting like a Neanderthal.

"When we get you back to town, I'll want to get an x-ray to make sure there is no other damage, but for now, we're going to drain the blood. That should help with the discomfort."

"Less discomfort would be nice." Mina smiled at him.

"A nice soak in warm salt water will help also." The doctor went about preparing to drain the accumulated blood. "How long will you be on the island?"

Mina looked to him.

"We don't know. We need to catch up with our ship in the next port."

The doctor nodded. "Any island will have plenty of warm salt water. Take a good soak whenever time allows."

"Will do." Mina kept her gaze on the syringe filling.

"When you return to your home, make sure to visit your

own physician. It wouldn't hurt to tell the ship's doctor what happened as well. I also want you to continue taking ibuprofen until you return home."

She nodded.

"It will help with the inflammation and prevent blood clots."

Again, she dipped her chin in a nod.

"Anything else we should do?" It wasn't really Kent's place to ask, but it never hurt to be fully aware. At least, aware in a different sense than he'd been all morning.

A banging on the door had Jo jumping off the sofa and stumbling across the expansive living area. The rapping sounded again. "Hold your horses."

"Who is it?" Ginnie blinked from the chair she'd fallen asleep in.

"I don't know yet." They'd been up until all hours of the morning trying unsuccessfully to not worry about their sister. Mina had always been the responsible one of the three. Not that she and Ginnie were irresponsible, it was just that sometimes Mina was almost more mother than sister. Even though Mina seemed to be trying to be less reserved on this trip, more spontaneous as she'd put it, for Mina to miss the boat was horribly out of character, and despite the crew reassuring them that people missed the ship's departure for all sorts of innocuous reasons, now that she and Jo had upgraded to an onboard phone plan, they couldn't help but worry about not only why did Mina miss the ship, but why wasn't she answering her phone.

On the other side of the cabin door, a man in a white uniform with shoulder epaulets held out a sheet of paper. "Good morning. Are you Miss Ummarino?"

Jo nodded.

"This is for you. We received the message just a little bit ago."

Unfolding the page, Jo quickly scanned the letter and

took her first easy breath since the ship sailed last evening. Spinning around, she waved the paper at her sister. "It's about Mina."

Sleepy eyes popped open wide as Ginnie sprang from her seat and ran to her sister. "What happened? Is she okay?"

"Yes." Jo handed her sister the note, and turned to thank the officer still standing at the door. "We appreciate your bringing this so quickly."

He tipped his head and smiling at her, mumbled, "My pleasure." She had the distinct feeling as she closed the door that he had not been referring to delivering the note.

A tight grip on the note, Ginnie continued to stare at the page. "I wonder if she hit her head?"

"What kind of a question is that?"

"Did you read the note?"

"Of course I did. All is well, they were delayed by a bicycle accident."

"And…"

"And what?"

"Read it again." Ginnie shoved the note back at her sister.

Jo scanned the page quickly. "Who is Ramon?"

"Oh, for the love of Pete." Ginnie threw her arms into the air. "Read it out loud."

"Delayed by bicycle accident. Everyone is fine. Mr. and Mrs. Harwood will meet up with ship in next port. Ramon Garza."

"So?"

"Mr. and Mrs. Harwood." Ginnie enunciated clearly. "They must have gotten married."

"What?" Jo looked at the note again. She'd skimmed over it so quickly that she'd missed the Mrs. attached to Kent's name. "Holy…."

"That's not quite what I'm thinking. I'm thinking she must have hit her head and married the guy."

"Or married him and then hit her head."

"What?" Ginnie rolled her eyes again.

"None of this makes sense."

Ginnie collapsed onto the sofa. "I know it happens all the time in Vegas. People get caught up in the excitement and the atmosphere—"

"And don't forget the booze. Lots of booze in Vegas."

"And you know this how?" Ginnie's head snapped around.

Jo smiled at her middle sister and shrugged. "Maybe it's a joke?"

"Some joke."

"Well, she has mentioned she wanted to be more adventurous. More spontaneous. Getting married to a near stranger, even if they did seem to be getting along well, would definitely fit the bill."

"So would ziplining!" In full Italian mode, Ginnie waved her arms as she paced. "There has to be a mistake. A misunderstanding. Right?"

"If it's not a mistake—if our sister did get caught up in the whole romance of the island—do they have wedding chapels on that island? I mean, wouldn't they need a license? A waiting period? Something?"

"I don't know. The tour guide didn't mention it. But all these Caribbean islands are popular for destination weddings." Ginnie collapsed onto the comfy sofa. "Could it really be?"

"Wow." Jo slid onto the sofa beside her sister and reached for the note. Reading it once again her eyes stumbled over the Mr. and Mrs. Harwood part. "Just wow."

"Kent's phone is still going straight to voice mail." Jim came through the cabin door, closing it behind him. "And wow what?"

Jo stretched out her hand with the note. "They got married."

"Who did?"

"Who. Who missed the ship yesterday? Kent and Mina. That's who."

"What?" Reading the short note, Jim sank into the chair across from them. "Oh, wow."

"Told ya." Ginnie leaned back and crossed her arms. "Now what?"

Jim shook his head. "Makes no sense at all. I know he's been talking about how happy his brother is now. And I suspected he was smitten with Mina, but to run off and get married himself?"

"Smitten?" Ginnie leveled her gaze with Jim's. "Do people still use that word?"

"I did." Jim smiled at her. "And I'm also thinking I'd better enjoy the next couple of night's sleep because I'll no doubt be relegated to the sofa when the newlyweds return."

"Newlyweds," Ginnie muttered. "This is really weird."

"That won't last for long." Jo sighed at her sister.

"Why do you say that?"

"Because when Mom finds out that her first daughter got married without her…" Jo let her words hang.

Ginnie's gaze widened. "Mom's going to kill her."

Jo nodded. "Or him."

"Oh, brother." Ginnie shook her head. "I think I need a drink."

"It's only nine o'clock in the morning."

"Our sister eloped with a practical stranger. Our older, responsible sister."

"You're right." Jo bobbed her head.

"She is?" Not unexpected that Jim would be surprised, they were teetotalers compared to his consumption skills.

"Not about the drink. That our sister must have hit her head."

"Which brings me around to my original question." Ginnie set the letter down on the coffee table. "Now what do we do?"

"How are you feeling now?"

Mina wiggled her fingers, delighted not to have the pain shooting up her arm. "It doesn't hurt as much."

"But it still hurts?" Concern was etched on Kent's face.

"It will." The doctor latched his bag shut. "What she tore in the fall still needs to heal."

"But it will heal?" The last thing Mina needed was to have some injury that required surgery to repair.

"It will. On that note, I'll be on my way." The doctor smiled at them and turned toward the door, Cecilia following behind.

Ramon took an empty seat at the table. "Now we decide what to do?"

"We should get into town. Arrange to get back to the ship." That was the logical next step. Though Mina wished she had clean clothes to shower and change into first.

"I checked with the port authority. Apparently, missing the boat is a common occurrence." Ramon chuckled. "There are six more passengers at the downtown hotel."

"You're kidding?" Mina couldn't believe that six others had also had bicycle accidents. "What made all those folks miss the boat?"

"I didn't ask, but I do know that there's a charter service that regularly flies passengers to whichever their cruise line's next port is. Your ship will not be at its next port until tomorrow."

Kent nodded. "It's a sea day today."

"You have to decide if you want to fly out later today or early tomorrow."

"You can decide after you freshen up." Cecilia held a pile of clothes in her arms. "You're about the same size as my daughter. One of these should fit. I'll wash your clothes now for you to wear back to the ship tomorrow."

"Tomorrow?" Kent asked.

"Well, yes." The grin on Cecilia's face seemed so matter-of-fact. "Why would you want to go stay in a strange hotel overnight, not to mention the expense, when you can wait it out here? Besides, the doctor said warm salt water would be good for you and we certainly have plenty of that." Cecilia folded her arms, her grin widening. "And we have lots of bathing suits for you to choose from."

Kent glanced at Mina.

Mina's surprise obviously showed on her face because Cecilia went on to explain. "When you live close to water the spare bathing suits start to accumulate to supply an entire family, and families come in all sizes. You get your choice of two piece, one piece, tankinis." She turned to Kent. "Sorry to say all you get is plain ordinary swim trunks."

Again, Kent looked to Mina. She could read in his eyes that he was leaving the decision to her. Then she saw by the slight nod of his head and uptick in the corners of his mouth when he knew what she'd decided. Had she ever dated anyone who could read her so easily? Lord knew she'd dated enough people who couldn't understand what she was thinking when she outright told them what was on her mind. This was something she could definitely get used to. *Used to*? What the hell was she talking about? She barely knew him, never mind was dating him. *Right*?

CHAPTER TWELVE

There were many things that appealed to Kent; walking along a sandy beach was most definitely one of them. Taking the stroll with Mina only made it better.

"How much further?" Mina called ahead to Ramon and Cecilia, who were holding hands and giggling like a couple of teens on a first date.

"Around this bend," Ramon called back.

"They look cute, don't they?" Wearing a large floppy hat Cecilia had given her, Mina smiled wistfully. "My parents look like that sometimes."

"Only sometimes?"

She shrugged. "Most of the time my parents aren't even in the same room together. The old school way of women in the kitchen and men somewhere else."

"Not always old school. Happens a lot in new school."

Her smile widened. "Don't get me wrong. That wasn't a complaint. My parents' home is always filled with people. Sometimes family, sometimes friends or neighbors, and often all of the above. There's always a lot of noise. Everyone talks at the same time, and if the room gets too loud to hear, everyone just talks louder." She chuckled. "But there's still always laughter, lots of love and plenty of fun. Even if the women shoo the men out of the kitchen."

"I bet the meals that come out of that kitchen are to die for."

"And then some. Mom and her sisters are the best cooks on the planet. My grandmother was a good teacher."

"Do you and your sisters cook too?"

This time she laughed even louder. "We'd be banned

from the family if we couldn't cook."

"I have a feeling all that love would be very tolerant if one of you couldn't cook as well as your mom."

Still smiling, Mina nodded. "Of course you're right. Anyhow. Every once in a blue moon, when the crowds lessen, we'll notice Mom and Dad smiling coyly at each other, or holding hands, or even stealing a kiss." She tipped her chin up toward Ramon and Cecilia. "Just like that."

He wished he could say the same about his parents. They spent more time fighting like the proverbial cat and dog than making nice. Of course it wasn't antagonistic all the time. As a matter of fact, now that he thought about it, his folks didn't bicker near as much as they had when he and his brother were growing up. Maybe they'd mellowed with age.

"Here we are." Ramon sat on a large crop of rocks and took off his shoes. "This is the only way to live."

His wife leaned over, kissed him on the nose and holding her hat on her head with one hand from a gust of wind, kicked her shoes off as well. "Hurry up. We have a little surprise for you."

"They really are a sweet couple." Kent had an unexpected urge to grab Mina's hand and keep walking the beach. "Can you imagine taking in two strangers not only overnight, but over two nights."

Mina chuckled. "Yeah, I can. As long as they don't look like axe murderers."

"And what exactly, if I may ask, do axe murderers look like?"

Kicking the water's edge as she walked, Mina tipped her head and glancing sideways at him, grinned. "Dangerous."

Kent burst out laughing. "Of course."

Only a short distance away from where Cecilia and Ramon had stopped by a large outcropping of rocks, Kent had taken his gaze off of Mina and took in where their hosts had gone. His mistake had been taking his eyes off of Mina. He turned to speak to her just in time to see her leaning over as a wave rushed ashore. The problem was he took too long to connect the dots that his sweet, responsible, and parental Mina wasn't merely leaning over to collect a shell, or feel the water. The woman cupped her hand, and in one fell swing of her arm, showered him with a large splash of salty water.

"Oh, now you're asking for it."

She took off at a fast trot, laughing and giggling, and slowing to scoop water with both hands, splashed him again. Clearly that elbow was feeling much better.

Running at near full speed, he scooped water in her direction as he nearly tripped over his own two feet and laughed as hard as she was.

"Nice try," she called, sprinting ahead and turning to splash him again.

Doubling his sprint speed, he used both hands to splash her, and when she slowed to return fire, he dove forward and scooped her up instead.

Caught by surprise, she squealed loudly, and then went back to laughing. "Put me down."

He held her out over the waves. "You sure about that?"

Her arms flew around his neck. "No!"

Spinning in place, he pretended to gather momentum to toss her into the waves.

"Kent Harwood. Don't. You. Dare."

He chuckled some more, enjoying holding her in his arms. He stared at her laughing eyes. "If I set you down, do we have a truce?"

"Hmm." She twisted her mouth to one side and looked contemplatively skyward. When he stretched forward holding her over the water again, she tightened her grip on him and practically screeched, "Truce!"

Still laughing, he carefully set her down. "I needed that."

"What?" She wiped the sand from her hands. "Threatening the fairer sex?"

Hands on his knees, taking deep breaths, he glanced up at her. "Laughing."

"Oh, that." She brushed her hands together and glanced over to where Ramon and Cecilia had disappeared. "We should probably go find them."

Still leaning over, catching his breath, he nodded then straightened. "Let's see what their surprise is." Sucking in one more deep breath, he decided to take a chance and held his hand out to her.

At first he wasn't sure if what he saw was confusion or concern, but when she stretched her hand and curled her fingers in his, he came within inches of doing a fist pump and giving a victory holler. He knew it wouldn't last long, but while it did, life was looking very good.

Mina could not remember the last time she laughed so hard. In truth, she couldn't remember the last time she'd had as much fun as she had, and not just a few minutes ago, but every minute that she had spent with Kent. Even being run off the road wasn't nearly so bad having him there with her. And just now, when he held out his hand to her, holding on just felt right.

"You two doing okay?" Cecilia popped her head up from above the rocks.

"Sorry," Kent shrugged apologetically, "we're coming."

Once they reached the outline of rocks that Ramon and Cecilia stood by, Mina realized that on the other side was a small cove reminiscent of the European grotto. The other thing she realized was that she didn't want to let go of Kent's hand.

"Oh, good." Ramon stood behind his wife. "Just in time."

Kent led the way up the rocks, still holding onto her hand. Rising up on one side of the landscape had been easy. Coming down the other side, she was grateful he had not let go of her hand.

"You may want to leave your shoes on high ground." Cecelia pointed in their direction.

Nodding, Mina took off her shoes and the oversized T-shirt she had over her swimsuit, and set them down on high ground. Following her hosts, she realized the water was almost like a private pool protected on three sides from the ocean waves.

As soon as they were over the rocks and in the cove, Kent let go of her hand. Of course she didn't need his help anymore. Hugging her sore arm against her chest, she followed Kent, walking to where Roman and Cecilia now stood, chest high, in the middle of the cove. The doctor had been right about one thing. As soon as the water washed over her injured elbow, the warmth and support was enough to almost make her forget it was hurt at all. Almost as much as the laughter.

"It's like our own private little hot springs." Cecilia tipped onto her back and looking up at the sun, floated in place.

"If you want to sit," Ramon pointed to the rear of the cove, "the depth grows more shallow as you retreat to the back and the closer you get to the mouth of the sea, the deeper it gets."

Mina nodded and digging her toes into the sand where she stood, tipped her face up to feel the warmth of the sun. Part of her wanted to float like Cecilia, another part of her wanted to keep her arm submerged in the warm water, and still another part, like a lost puppy, wanted to follow Kent wherever he went.

"And here they come." As soon as Ramon spoke, his wife shifted upright and came to stand beside him.

"You're going to love this." Cecilia grinned at them.

Not sure what the couple was talking about, Mina looked over the rocks from the direction they'd come for visitors. No one in sight. She turned her head back toward Kent wondering who was here when she spotted the movement in the water. Another few seconds and she made out a small fin sticking out of the water. The landlocked city girl she was, immediately thought shark. Then common sense slowly took over as she processed that no one became as enthusiastic as their hosts over sharks. It had to be a dolphin.

No sooner had she managed to breathe again at her

revelation than just outside the entrance to the cove, a dolphin sprang up in the cove and did what looked like a perfect pirouette before splashing back into the water. And that was when Mina realized she wasn't watching one or two dolphins but perhaps a whole family and a few friends as well. "Wow."

She might have been the one to mutter her astonishment, but the wide-eyed smile on Kent's face showed he was as surprised and impressed with the friendly visitors as she was.

"Hello, Miss Margaret," Ramon said softly to a dolphin swimming around him. Mina wasn't completely sure but, it looked to her like the dolphin had singled Ramon out and tipped sideways to give Ramon a hello splash.

As Ramon interacted with Miss Margaret, another dolphin circled around her.

"They won't hurt you." Cecilia smiled. "That's Herman, Margaret's mate."

More dolphins made their way into the cove, until four or five were swimming around them, bumping the back of their legs or nudging their hips. Every few minutes one of them would swim away and then come back flipping and splashing beside them. Never had Mina had so much fun getting drenched.

"Do they all have names?" Kent asked, his arms at his side.

"We only recognize Margaret and Herman. Margaret has a little notch in her top fin. Herman has a scar on his nose." Cecilia pointed at each. "We first met Margaret when she had a net stuck on her fin. Ramon cut her loose."

"Then, not long after that, Margaret came to visit, swimming crazy in circles. Ramon followed her and Herman was trapped in a fisherman's line that wouldn't break. He wasn't in good shape."

"Ramon cut him loose too?"

Cecilia nodded. "And we've all been good friends ever since. I'm always surprised that they seem to know when we're here." Cecilia splashed with one of the dolphins then glanced up at Mina. "Do you like your surprise?"

Head bobbing like a kid's toy, she grinned. "Very much."

One dolphin in particular, at least she thought it was the same one, swam back and forth, carefully brushing against her hip every time he or she passed.

"He knows you're hurt," Ramon called from across the cove. "That's why he's being extra careful around you."

"Aren't you sweet."

"If you open your palm and drop your hand into the water, he'll probably come up to you and bump your hand with his nose."

"Really?" Sucking in a deep breath, Mina spread her fingers and placed her good hand in the water. Sure enough, within minutes her new friend came swimming up to her and bumped her hand with his nose. But to make matters even more fun, right after he bumped her hand he sprang up straight and backed up, shaking his head and making the cutest dolphin noise. It was as if he were congratulating her for shaking hand and nose. "Amazing," she muttered softly. *Just amazing.*

Having only one good arm left Mina at a distinct disadvantage. While Kent and the others were diving and swimming and truly playing with all the visitors, she simply stood in the middle of the cove grinning like the village idiot at the dolphins swimming around her. For a moment her mind shifted to her sisters on the ship. She wondered how Jo's scuba efforts were going and if Jo was having as much fun as they were. Maybe the kid was right and scuba diving wasn't such an awful thing. In all honesty, she'd always thought she'd led a pleasant, full life, but she was pretty sure nothing she'd ever done had been as much fun as playing with dolphins.

In the middle of all the giggles and laughing and splashing, one of the dolphins sprang up and landed with a splash at her side, seconds later Kent did the same. Springing up from under the water like a geyser, sidling up beside her, he shook his head like a wet dog and showered her with warm salt water. Laughter overrode the urge to screech at the unexpected dousing.

Wiping the water from his face, Kent stood at her side. "How you doing?"

"Great."

"This is one heck of a way to spend an afternoon."

"Gives lots of motivation to retire on an island away from the rest of the world."

"Agreed." Tipping his head in her direction, he shook his hair at her again, sprinkling water in her face. "Still want to retire on a small island?"

She nodded. "Most definitely." As a matter of fact, if today could last forever, she'd take it.

CHAPTER THIRTEEN

The cab parked in front of the house bright and early to whisk Mina and Kent to the small island airport. In the distance, the morning sun danced on the ocean.

Kent swallowed the last sip of his coffee. So many things about this place, these people, were going to be hard to forget. Especially one in particular. "A penny for your thoughts?"

"The sunrise is so beautiful. I'm torn between the need to get back to my sisters and the desire to stay here getting to know everyone better."

He could certainly understand that, but as far as he was concerned, there was only one person he really wanted to know better. Though if he were honest with himself, he already knew enough about Mina Ummarino to know she mattered to him. A lot. The question was what was he going to do about it.

"It's been lovely having you with us." Cecilia stood in the open doorway. "If you're ever back this way again, look us up."

"Will do. I promise." Mina leaned in and gave her hostess with the mostest a kiss on the cheek. "We had a wonderful visit. Thank you."

"Yes." Kent stuck his hand out to shake with Ramon. "I wish we could stay longer. If you're ever stateside, you make sure to call."

Even though their hosts nodded and agreed, he knew they'd probably never see each other again. He also knew he would never forget a single thing about the last two days.

He waved an arm toward the cab. "Ready?"

"Not really, but let's go."

Settled in the backseat, they waved at their former hosts standing in the doorway until the small house and the two people disappeared from view.

"I'm going to miss them." Kent leaned his head back. "And this place." And in a few more days, the company at his side too.

"I wonder how Jo and Ginnie are doing?"

"They're probably having a ball. Especially Jo with her scuba lessons."

Mina laughed. "I actually forgot about that. I wonder if she roped Ginnie into joining her."

"Do you think she might have?"

She shrugged. "Normally I'd say no, but after the last couple of days I think I have a better understanding of expect the unexpected."

"True."

The cab came around the bend and the small port town came into view. "I thought town was farther away."

"When you're in a car everything seems closer. It's when we have to walk that it's so far away."

Mina chuckled. "You do have a point there."

"You want to try to buy a phone before we get back on the ship?" Kent asked.

"I thought about it. But overall, we're going to be together and reception seems to be a challenge more often than not. I might as well wait till I get on the ship and buy it there."

Kent nodded. "Then we're off."

The cab driver pulled into a small parking area outside the open air terminal. On the tarmac one plane in particular caught his eye. Not since his trip to the Big Island had he seen a commercial aircraft parked with a rollaway ladder in front of the airplane door. It was easy to forget that modern gangways with airplanes unloading people directly into the airport terminal were not commonplace worldwide.

They had less than an hour before their flight left so they didn't waste any time in the small terminal. Once they'd settled up with the bike rental place and paid for their seats on the plane, Mina paused a time or two at a kiosk to glance at some of the souvenirs sold by the locals.

"I wish I had thought to offer to buy some of Ramon's driftwood pieces."

"Look on the bright side, it gives you an excuse to come back and bring your sisters."

The corners of her mouth tipped upward in a sweet smile. "I wonder if they have a nice hotel in this town?"

"Do you really think if you were to come visit with your sisters Ramon and Cecilia would let you guys stay in a hotel?"

Mina threw her arms up in the air and laughed. "What could I have been thinking?"

The loudspeaker overhead called the passengers to board the plane. Keeping her small backpack with her, Mina led the way. The flight was short. They barely had time to take off, hit a few patches of turbulence, and then land at their ship's next stop. In many ways most of the islands looked very much the same: lots of greenery, lots of colorful housing, plenty of beachfront, and warm ocean breezes.

Nonetheless, this port town was a bit bigger than where they had just come from. Kent glanced at his watch. "The ship should be docking within the hour."

"Actually," Mina held her hand over her brow, "I know lots of ships stop at this port but I think that one out in the distance is ours."

Kent followed the direction of her gaze, and nodded. "I think you may be right. I can see the ocean view lounge at the back of the boat."

"You know," Mina turned to face him, her hand still over her brow, her grin a little brighter, "I'm actually even more excited than I was when we first decided to take the cruise."

"Really, how?"

"In my wildest dreams, I could not have imagined how yesterday would have turned out. Even though I'd rather not have any more crazy accidents, I'm really looking forward to what the rest of this cruise has in store for us."

For us. He liked the sound of that. Though he doubted she was referring to him and her. Most likely, the us was her and her sisters. Too bad. He really liked the idea of being part of an us. Much more than he ever thought he would.

"What does it say?" Jo stood behind her sister, looking over her shoulder at the message another steward had delivered. Apparently ship to shore communications worked much better for the cruise line than passenger's cell phones did.

"Not much." Ginnie handed the paper the steward had delivered to her.

*So much to tell you. Great couple of days. See you
in port today.*

"Doesn't say much, does it?" Jo handed it back to her sister.

Ginnie stared at the page frowning. "Great couple of days. As in honeymoon days?"

"Well," Jo shrugged, "I'm wondering about what *so much* is she going to tell us. As in why the heck she missed the boat, or as in why the heck did she get married without us there?"

"Do you really think they got married?" Ginnie continued to study the page as if the paper would magically begin speaking to her. "Without us?"

"I don't know. It makes no sense to me either, but we're docked. They'll let us off the ship soon. Should we wait here for her or meet her somewhere in port?"

Ginnie shook her head. "No clue."

"Do you think Jim knows anything more?"

"He got in pretty late last night. I wouldn't expect to see him any time soon."

"I didn't get in that late." Jim smiled at the two sisters and scratching the back of his head roughly, yawned loudly. "I'm in desperate need of caffeine."

"Room service brought us a carafe." Ginnie pointed to the coffee table. "It might still be warm."

"Thanks." Jim sat on the sofa and fixed himself a cup of the still warm, though not quite hot, coffee. "This hits the spot."

"Have you heard from Kent?" Jo sat in the chair across from him.

He shook his head. "Nothing since the odd message we got telling us they were safe."

A rap sounded at the cabin door. Since she was the only one standing, Ginnie crossed the short distance and opened the door. On the other side, a large bouquet of flowers greeted her. From behind the flowers, a male voice announced, "Delivery for Mr. and Mrs. Harwood."

The words had Jo's head snapping around to meet Ginnie's startled gaze.

Shaking her head, Ginnie snapped herself into the moment. "Thank you. I'll take them."

The steward handed her the flowers.

"Is there a note?" Jo followed her sister to the table she set the flowers on. "What does it say?"

Ginnie glared at her sister. "Will you give me a minute, please?"

Now Jim was on his feet, also looking over Ginnie's shoulder. "I'm with Jo. What does it say?"

Dearest Mina and Kent, it was an absolute joy having you here the last couple of days. Wishing you a lovely rest of your trip and hope you come back again some day soon. All our best, Ramon and Cecilia.

Jo looked at the envelope the note came with. "Mr. and Mrs. Harwood."

"I guess that answers all our questions." Jim whistled softly. "I still can't believe they got married. How did I miss they liked each other that much?"

Ginnie stared at the flowers. "They tracked each other when they thought no one was looking."

"What?" Jo had absolutely no idea what the heck her sister was talking about.

Fingering the name on the envelope, Ginnie turned to face her sister. "I noticed that first day at sea. They tracked each other. Whenever they thought we weren't looking, Kent followed Mina's movements and visa versa. I knew there was interest, but I didn't see this coming."

"Mom is going to have a cow."

"If she doesn't have a stroke first." Ginnie sucked in a deep breath then blew it out and plastered on a big smile. "Whatever their reasons, we have some work to do before they come on board."

"We do?" Once again, Jo had no clue where her sister was going with this.

"We do!" Ginnie slapped her hands together and rubbed them with more enthusiasm than Jo understood. "I'll call down to the concierge." She spun around and waved a finger at Jim. "And you get dressed. I don't know how much time we have so let's get moving!"

Jim and Jo stared at Ginnie dialing down to the main desk. Whatever her sister had in mind, she was in full command mode. Heaven help anyone who got in her way.

"There she is." Mina pointed to the ship in port. "She looks prettier than I remembered."

Kent chuckled. "If you say so."

"You know what I mean." The ship was docked but they weren't letting passengers off or on. From what they'd seen, only delivery personnel were being allowed aboard so far, and not many of those at that. "After missing it the other day, it's nice to be back."

He nodded. "Yeah, I know what you mean. Though I'm not looking forward to running into Jim. He's going to tease me mercilessly about missing the ship."

"Why? It wasn't your fault."

"No, but he told me not to book a private excursion.

Had we been on a ship sponsored tour, the ship would have waited for the group.”

“Maybe.” She thought back to the last two days. “I don’t think I would have traded our stay with Ramon and Cecilia.” Or her time getting to know Kent better.

Around the port authority building, kiosks were opening up, preparing for the onslaught of tourists with plenty of money to spend on trinkets and other souvenirs. At the opposite end of the building Kent spied a small café. “Shall we grab a cup of coffee while we wait?”

Tearing her gaze away from the ship, she glanced in the same direction he pointed in. “If you don’t mind, I’d rather wait here. I’m sure they’re going to let us on the ship very soon.”

“Fine with me.” He gestured to a bench near the railing that separated the port town from the dock. They’d barely made it to the bench when the security personnel began moving about and setting up at different stations.

“Looks like the flood of tourists is about to descend on us.”

She pulled out her ID and key card. “Shall we see if they let us on?”

“All ready.” Their cards in hand, she followed Kent to the first security guard at the rail. From there, they proceeded to two more guards before reaching the final doorway to the docks and meeting the ship’s representative.

“Mr. Harwood. Good to see you made it back.”

Kent nodded. “Can we board yet?”

The man nodded. “Yes, the ship is expecting you. Though at this hour it may be a bit like a fish swimming up stream when everyone else is coming downstream.”

“I think we’ll manage.” Kent turned to her and smiled. “Honey, we’re home.”

Mina burst out laughing, clicked her heels together and repeated, “There’s no place like home.”

At the first podium, they slowed only to have the ship staff direct them to the gangway further down the dock.

“I guess this is better than swimming upstream.” Kent eased his hand at her lower back and nudged her forward.

No surprise that Mina wished he'd kept his hand there a little longer.

At the next entry point, he showed his card and the crew member looked at him so long that she wondered what he was expecting to see. The crewman inserted the card, read the screen in front of him and then to Mina's relief, the man smiled. "Welcome aboard, Mr. Harwood. Glad to see you back."

"Thank you." Kent moved forward to let Mina hand over her keycard.

The man smiled at her without expressing the same serious scrutiny he'd given Kent a moment ago. "Here you go, Mrs. Welcome back."

Mina nodded, not seeing the point in correcting she was a Miss not a Mrs. She was even more surprised when Kent reached back and extending his arm, grabbed hold of her hand. It took a full minute more before he looked down at their joined hands and seemed as surprised as she was that he'd taken hold of it. But even more of a surprise was that once he realized what he'd done, he didn't try to let go. Instead, he waited for her reaction, and since she had no intention of letting go, he smiled and tugged her forward.

Even though they'd entered on the opposite end of the ship, the clutter of people had them maneuvering past those on line trying to depart and the path to the elevators. A plethora of tourists coming and going, ready for a day of sightseeing and fun. Nothing out of the ordinary, nothing different. It struck Mina as almost surreal. They'd been gone for two days and everything felt so different in so many ways, and yet, here on the ship, everything seemed very much the same.

"Where do you think your sisters are?" Kent pressed the up button for the elevator.

"Good question. Let's start at the promenade so I can pick up a new phone, then we can hit the room. If they're not in the room, at least I'll have a new phone to call them with."

"Makes sense. I'll plug mine in as soon we get to the room. If Jim isn't there, I can text him in a few. I doubt he'll be as concerned about me as your sisters will be about you."

The elevators to the promenade deck opened and Mina could hear the music playing louder than usual. As she turned the corner, she could see the small band in the atrium playing, but unlike the usual fare the steel bands played, she could swear they were playing Here Comes the Bride.

"Sounds like someone is getting married." Ken was still holding her hand and looking around at the crowds, studying those stopping to study the band on their way off the ship.

Mina looked at the people standing nearby, not a single one dressed like a bride. "I wonder who's getting married?"

CHAPTER FOURTEEN

Something was off and Kent couldn't quite put his finger on it. He also didn't know how long he could get away with holding on to Mina, but when she didn't seem to mind the gesture, a ripple of excitement made itself at home deep inside him. He had no idea what the next few days at sea held, but he was looking forward to finding out.

A waiter came to stop beside them, extending a tray with champagne flutes. "Champagne, Mimosa, Poinsettia?"

"Poinsettia?" Mina leaned against Kent. "He doesn't mean the Christmas plant, does he?"

Kent stifled a chuckle. "Champagne and cranberry juice."

"Oh." Mina smiled. "I'll try one of those."

Taking a traditional orange juice and champagne Mimosa, Kent took in the other waiters offering the curious bystanders a morning drink. "I guess we're going to toast the bride and groom."

Other passengers were sipping and watching. The band switched to another popular wedding song and still no sign of the bride and groom.

"Do you think they're even here?" Mina took a small sip of her drink. "Ooh. This is delicious."

"There they are!" Jo's voice could be heard over the murmuring crowd.

From across the atrium, Jo and Ginnie waved madly as they cut through the crowd, finally reaching the third sister, and expertly balancing their champagne glasses, the three did a massive group hug worthy of an absence much longer than a couple of days.

"We missed you!" Jo shouted over the music, her jaw dropping open at the sight of her arm in a sling. "You're hurt! What happened?"

"I had a little mishap with a speeding car—"

"You were hit by a car!" Ginnie's jaw fell open and her eyes circled around showing the whites of her eyes.

"Relax. The car didn't hit me but I did take a bit of a fall. The bike didn't survive."

Jo shook her head. "Stupid drivers." Her gaze shifted to their intertwined hands and the worried look slid away, replaced by a sappy smile. "Isn't that cute."

As if her sister's words held a bolt of electricity, Mina's cheeks flushed a lovely shade of pink and she hurriedly let go of Kent's hand.

Immediately, Jo scooped her sister's free hand in her own and looking at her fingers frowned. "You're not wearing a ring?"

Returning her sister's curious frown, Mina shook her head.

Ginnie batted her younger sister's hand away and squeezed Mina's hand. "Don't listen to her. Tell us all about it."

"Yeah," Jo agreed. "Don't skip any details."

Shaking her head, Ginnie elbowed her sister. "I could do without *every* detail."

"Oh." Jo giggled. "I guess you're right."

"Hey, bro." Jim slapped Kent on the back. "Well done."

Something in the tone of his friend's voice didn't sit right. "I didn't do much."

Jim chuckled. "Right."

It was obvious to Kent that Jim clearly thought they'd shared a torrid time on the island. "You're incorrigible."

"Hey," Jim tipped his head and hefted a lazy shoulder, "I'm not the one who's full of surprises."

Ginnie grinned at her sister. "There's going to be a little reception on the upper deck. Nothing too fancy."

"That's nice." Mina smiled back, despite the wonderful time she'd had, pleased to be back on the ship and reunited with her sisters. "Are you guys going?"

"Are we going?" Jo's blue eyes popped open wide. "Of course. It's bad enough we missed the wedding."

"Oh." Mina looked at Kent, her gaze seemed to be asking if he was having as much trouble following the sister's train of thought. He gave her the slightest nod of his head and was rewarded with a super sweet smile and a quick squeeze of his hand before she let go again.

The two sisters were rambling on about a cake and change of clothes, but Kent's attention was on Mina. A tumbleweed of emotions swirled inside him. So little time had passed and yet so much had changed. He was confronted with feelings as foreign to him as a distant continent and didn't know how to begin unraveling the emotions building in him. All he knew is he very much wanted to hold Mina's hand again, and slip away from her gushing siblings who behaved as if their two day mishap on a tropical island had been more akin to a two year absence in a terrorist occupied jungle.

"You guys may want to freshen up." Ginnie gestured at the two of them. "We'll meet you on the upper deck."

"Yeah." Jo nodded and winked. "This way you can have a little privacy."

"Not too much privacy." Ginnie waved a finger. "The party starts in twenty minutes." Almost shaking with excitement, Ginnie leaned in and squeezed her sister again. "I'm so happy for you. See you upstairs."

Ginnie locked elbows with Jo and tugged her away.

"I'd better go with them." Jim sighed. "Fortunately, the sofa pulls out in the living room."

"What?" Kent must have lost track of key points in the multiple conversations going on.

"Unless I can find a better offer." Jim raised his hand palms out. "Don't bother telling me to keep my distance from the sisters. I'm working on the cute blonde. Will keep you posted."

From several feet ahead, Ginnie looked over her shoulder and blew a clear, not too loud whistle. "Joining us, Jim?"

It may have come out like a question but it was clear to anyone watching that her words bore more resemblance to an order than a request. The three ran off like a couple of kids with a fist full of candy money.

"Do you think they've completely lost their minds?" Mina kept her gaze on her siblings.

"Maybe it's too much sun."

Mina nodded. "Maybe. Or maybe they started drinking champagne too early this morning."

"More champagne, Mrs.?" A waiter stopped at her side.

Mina snapped her head around to look at the waiter, then held up her half full flute. "No, thank you."

The guy smiled and moved on to the next passenger.

"I wonder if I should tell him that he should be saying ma'am, not Mrs."

"I don't think it matters."

"No. I suppose you're right." Mina sighed. "I guess we'd better go freshen up. I don't want to disappoint them."

He extended his hand to her palm up.

Mina's gaze dropped to his hand, and then leveled with his. Her eyes twinkling, she smiled and wrapped her fingers around his. The warmth of her hand in his made his chest swell with contentment and something more. As crazy as the thought was, he was beginning to think all the fuss over some couple tying the knot on the cruise wasn't such a crazy idea. It actually felt like a really good idea. That or he was completely losing his mind. Only the next few days would prove which was the truth.

Mina didn't have a clue what had brought on all the hand holding, but she was almost as giddy about the contact as her sister was about the wedding party upstairs. Maybe more.

As soon as the door was open, the first thing Mina spotted was the gorgeous floral arrangement on the coffee table. "Oh my, that's beautiful." Noticing the card beside the vase, she read the short note from Ramon and Cecilia out loud.

"That was very sweet of them." Kent stood at the bar. "I think the ship has an obsession with champagne."

Not only was there another ice bucket with champagne chilling, from where she stood, she could also see a large tray of chocolate covered strawberries. Up close, the tray was even bigger than the one the day they had arrived. "I wonder what we did to deserve this again?"

"Maybe it's an every other day sort of thing?" Kent shrugged.

Mina picked up the card beside the strawberries. "*Congratulations*." She showed the card to Kent. "I wonder what went on while we were gone?"

Kent took the folded note from her. "Maybe this has something to do with Jo's scuba classes?"

"Of course." She nodded. "That makes perfect sense."

"I don't know about you," Kent set the card down on the bar, "but right about now, that hot tub on the deck is looking way more appealing than any party with a bunch of rabble-rousers out in the sun."

She knew exactly what he meant. Especially if it meant soaking in the warm water with him at her side. "My sisters would probably kill me if we don't show up. For whatever reason they were very excited about this little party."

He sidled up next to her, and facing her, took her good hand in both of his. "Rain check?"

Standing so close, the warmth of his hands radiating up her arms, joining her sisters held even less appeal than it had a minute ago. Slowly, she nodded. "Rain check."

Before she could even think about moving, his lips pressed ever so softly against hers. The sweetest, most tender kiss. She wasn't sure who moved first, or when he let go of her hand, but now she stood toe to toe, his arms gently wrapped around her, her one arm looped around his neck, the other pressed between them, she was completely lost in his kiss.

The ringing of a phone broke the spell she'd fallen under. Easing back, Kent blew out a stuttered sigh. "I suppose one of us should answer that."

"Somebody has terrible timing."

Kent muffled a small chuckle. "I won't argue with you. Right about now I have an overwhelming urge to lock all the doors."

This time Mina chuckled. "I don't think my sisters would appreciate that."

"I'm more concerned about how you feel." There was a softness in his voice that had her knees turning to mush.

"I'd better answer the phone." She stepped away and reached for the landline across the room. "Hello."

"Don't you two get distracted. The party is about to start," Ginnie admonished.

"I know. We're coming." Hanging up, Mina shook her head and turned toward her room. "That was Ginnie. I'd better hurry."

Still standing in place, Kent nodded.

It took Mina all of 20 seconds to notice none of her clothes were in the closet. "That's strange." She had to wonder if her sister would've sent all of her clothes out to be laundered. That made no sense at all. She opened her designated drawers. Nothing. *What the heck.* She crossed into the living room. "Something very strange is going on."

"Not so strange." Kent now stood by the champagne bottle holding a piece of paper. "I think this explains a lot." He handed her a small envelope. "I'm guessing the card you read by the strawberries came in this envelope."

Mina looked down. "Mr. and Mrs. Harwood?"

"How much do you want to bet that wedding reception upstairs is for us?"

Pivoting around, she collapsed in the nearest chair, and stared at the envelope again before looking over to the bar and then back to Kent. "Good grief. They think we're married."

CHAPTER FIFTEEN

Perhaps Kent was jumping to conclusions, but the odd way the sisters and Jim were acting could be explained if they thought he and Mina had eloped on the island.

"I guess there's only one way to find out." Mina pushed to her feet. "I'll be dressed in a minute."

Kent nodded at her and took a step toward his room when she stopped in her tracks.

"Except," she turned to face him, "where are my clothes?"

He sucked in a breath. Functioning on the assumption everyone thought they were married, he hurried into his room and opened the closet door. "I think I found them."

"What about Jim?"

"This," he waved at the closet, "would explain what Jim meant by the couch comment."

"So we just need to tell them the truth and return our worlds to normal again."

He nodded. Made perfectly good sense, but a niggling tickle deep in his gut told him some things were easier said than done.

Already he had a growing list of things he really loved about Mina. Loved. Wasn't that a hoot. A figure of speech common in all aspects of life. *I love that sunset, I love double chocolate chip cookies, I love summer.* When it came to Mina, he really loved the twinkle in her eyes when she laughed, the way she got excited with something new, her willingness to try new things, her ability to stay calm under fire, and now, that she could shower and dress and be ready to go in as little time as it took him to get out the door. How could any man resist a woman like that. Heaven knew he couldn't resist her and his feelings for her had nothing to do with a figure of speech. He was falling head over heels for Philomena Ummarino.

"Ready to face the music?" Mina stood in the doorway in a royal blue sundress and flat strappy sandals that made her legs look long, lean, and impossible to keep his eyes away from. "Everything okay?"

The look of honest concern on her face had his heart doing a back flip. This was some serious emotion kicking around inside him. "Everything is fine…" he flashed his best smile. "Mrs. Harwood."

Mina burst out laughing, and shook her head. "How did this mess ever get started?"

"I don't know, but we'd better go fix it." He extended his elbow to her.

"Why, thank you kind sir," her voice danced with a fake southern accent.

Intending to escort her upstairs, he couldn't resist spinning her into him by her good arm until she was up close and personal. Like he'd done only a little while ago, he pulled her closely against him and once again let his lips dance over hers. A sweet melding of flesh and yearning that he would gladly indulge for the rest of the night—that is, if the world wasn't waiting for them on the upper deck. As he'd reluctantly done earlier, he eased back, this time simply staring into her eyes, admiring the beautiful depths. "This might be a hard habit to break."

Her smile widened. "I'm counting on it." Still wrapped in the hold of his arms, Mina didn't seem to be in any hurry to move. Not even when the cabin door creaked open.

"See? I told you we couldn't leave them alone." Ginnie nudged her younger sister into the room, and tapping her foot, dropped her fisted hands onto her hips, leaving her elbows waving in the breeze like a pair of chicken wings. "The ship is nice enough to throw this little shindig for you, the least you guys can do is cooperate just enough to show up."

"About that." Kent stepped back, but rather then let go

of her the way they'd done previously, he turned far enough to tuck her into his side. "We're not married."

Happily ensconced into Kent's side, Mina almost missed the color drain from her sister's face as Ginnie rocked in place.

"You're not?"

Like matching bobble heads, Mina and Kent shook their heads left then right then back again.

"But the notes," Jo stammered, her brows buckled in confusion.

"A mistake," Kent provided.

"Mistake?" The confusion on Ginnie's face shifted to irritation. "How does anyone make a mistake like that?"

Mina shrugged. "Ramon and Cecilia assumed we were married. I guess there was never a good time to correct them."

"The same could be said for the cruise line. I'm sure it was no skin off the chef's nose to bake you a small cake, and the bands are on board and playing all the time anyhow, but still it was very thoughtful of them when they learned of the impromptu wedding to provide a little reception."

"More likely, they want to win us over so we don't demand a refund, or worse, sue over the cabin snafu." Kent shrugged but didn't let go of Mina.

Jo fell into the nearby chair. "You're really not married?"

Mina and Kent shook their heads and shrugged. "Afraid not."

"This isn't a terrible joke?" Jo asked.

Mina shook her head again, then made an X over her chest with her finger. "Cross my heart."

"So now what do we do?" Jo looked from one sister to the other.

"We don't have much choice." Mina blew out a sigh. "We go upstairs, smile, nod, drink champagne, eat cake and then come back here and move my clothes back into our closet."

"We don't tell them?" Jo frowned.

All of her life Mina did her best not to lie, not even little white ones, but right now, they didn't have much choice. At least not without putting cruise line and family in an embarrassing predicament.

Most of the guests who'd opted to stay on board and now lingered on the upper deck seemed oblivious to who the newlyweds might be. The cake was little more than a rectangular white sheet cake with red roses on one side and a typical bride and groom cake topper. Based on the already sliced pieces of cake on the table, Mina suspected this particular cake was for show and the rest were being cut up in the kitchen. As long as no one asked them to feed each other, all should go well.

Less than thirty minutes later the cruise director stood to one side, microphone in hand, and proceeded to not only announce the non-existent marriage, he called them out for a dance as man and wife.

"Maybe coming up here was a mistake," Mina mumbled to no one in particular.

"I'm kind of glad to have another excuse to hold you."

She wasn't sure what she'd expected him to say, but that wasn't it. Swallowing hard, she managed to look him in the eyes. "Me too."

"Then shall we, Mrs. Harwood?"

The twinkle in his eyes made her smile. "Let's."

For a band, that before today, she'd only heard playing Caribbean rhythms, they did an excellent job of playing Al Green's *Let's Stay Together*. The slow melody seemed to wrap them in their own little world. She hadn't noticed how perfectly they fit together. Never had being in a man's arms felt so right. She wasn't the best of dancers, but following his lead, she felt like Ginger Rogers. Floating on air, swaying as one with him, she let her head nestle into his shoulder. "Can we stay here forever?"

"It's a thought. Though we might have to stop for food and water."

"Sustenance is over-rated."

Kent chuckled and somehow pulled her in closer. "Maybe no one will notice if we stay here and dance until we return to Miami."

She mumbled into his shoulder, "Works for me."

The song came to an inevitable end and a different member of the entertainment staff called them out to cut the cake.

"Be gentle with me," he teased as she sliced into the cake.

"Never mind gentle, just be good."

Each of them held a small piece of cake in their hands. She went first, gently placing a small morsel in his mouth. The onlookers cheered, watching their every move. Her turn was next. For a split second, a mischievous twinkle appeared in Kent's eyes and she thought she was going to wind up with frosting up her nose. Instead, his gaze deepened and the moment her lips closed around the cake and his fingers, his face came closer and he kissed a dabble of frosting away from the corner of her mouth. "Good?" he whispered.

"Very," she answered.

The same crewmember announced the upcoming line up of afternoon activities and just like that, the marital celebration was over.

"That wasn't so hard at all." Jo came up beside them. "But you guys put on one heck of a show."

"Agreed." Ginnie came up beside her sister. "I had no idea you were that good an actress, Mina."

Mina shrugged. Truth was there was no need to act. As absurd as the entire idea was, she was most definitely head over sandals falling for one Kent Harwood.

"I don't know about you two, but all this champagne and cake has actually left me hungry for real food. Last one to the buffet is a rotten egg." Jo turned to Ginnie. "You hungry too?"

Ginnie bobbed her head. "Famished. I skipped breakfast moving Mina's things into the other room and coordinating the little surprise with the staff. I could eat a whale."

"I wonder where Jim is?"

And just like that, Ginnie and Jo disappeared in the crowd of sunbathers crossing the deck.

"Are you hungry too?" Kent asked her.

"Not really." Not for food anyhow, but she wasn't going to tell him that.

"Listen." His hand on her lower back, he eased her away from the throngs of people and over to a quiet corner, then leaned against the railing. "I know this is a bit presumptuous of me, but I want to make something clear before your sisters throw more things at us."

Unsure of where he was going with this, she nodded and willed her nerves to chill out.

"I know these boats are famous for short flings."

She nodded, steeling herself for bad news.

"I don't know what we have going on here right now, but I know one thing."

Sucking in a deep breath, she nodded, silently urging him to go on.

"I don't want whatever we have going for us to end when the cruise ends."

And just like that the butterflies in her stomach stopped flapping their broad wings and sheer delight moved into its place.

"I want to see you when we get home. Often."

"I think I'm going to like that. A lot."

"Really?" The corners of his lips tipped upward and not till the twinkle returned to his eyes did she realize he'd been as nervous about what he'd said as she'd been waiting for him to say it.

"Really." She returned his smile. "And for the record, I'm very glad your brother and sister-in-law and the cruise line botched this. Very glad."

This time, he did the nodding. "I'm going to have to remember to send them something special when we get home. Though I don't think there's anything I could do that would be enough to thank them for bringing you into my life."

She didn't get a chance to respond. His lips met hers in

a short but telling kiss that held promises for things to come. Definitely owed her neighbor big time.

Kent straightened to his full height and taking hold of her good hand, smiled. "Shall we go put the cabin back the way it should be, Mrs. Harwood?"

"Love to, Mr. Harwood."

EPILOGUE

"Have you ever seen two happier people?" Jo and Mina's mother smiled brighter than the Cheshire Cat.

"I'm telling you," the sisters' neighbor Angie waved an arm at her neighbors' mother, "cruise ships and love seem to go hand-in-hand."

Antoinette Ummarino stopped stirring her sauce. "If that's true, how come only one daughter came home with a man?"

Chuckling, Angie shrugged. "Maybe there's a one romance per ship quota."

"I just want my girls to be happy. All of them. A good man, children, a nice home, and life will be good."

"Mama," Jo kissed her mother on the cheek, "life is good for all of us. Modern women don't need men and children to be happy."

Her mother shrugged. "Maybe not, but it doesn't hurt. Look at how happy your sister is."

Arguing with her mother was not an option. Even when the woman wasn't right, she was never wrong. And Jo had to hand it to her mom, Mina never looked happier. Even Kent, despite not having a drop of Italian blood in him, fit in beautifully with their loud and lively family. Of course much of that probably had to do with how much he obviously loved Mina and less with his love for the family in general. Jo wasn't exactly sure what happened on those two days on the island; well, that wasn't totally true. She did know about the bike accident, and the delicious dinner, and swimming with the dolphins, but she didn't know the rest. Her older sister was still her sister, but something had shifted and it was more than having fallen in love. For one thing, no one had been more shocked than Jo when Mina opted to join the scuba class and actually went underwater with the rest of them the last day of the cruise. Surely that wasn't love's fault?

"Is that onion pizza I smell?" Nose in the air, Jo's father came into the kitchen, sniffing out the delicious aromas like a bloodhound on a mission. "It is."

Shaking her head, Antoinette Ummarino rolled her eyes at her husband and did a miserable job of hiding a flattered smile. "You've been smelling my pizza for over thirty years."

Her father slid one arm around his wife's waist and with his free hand pinched a section of olive oil drizzled onions and moaned with delight before kissing his wife on the cheek. "And I love it almost as much as I love you."

"There they go again," Jo teased, her gaze drifting to the back patio where her sister and if she was any judge of people, her soon-to-be future brother-in-law, stood in almost a mirror image of her parents.

"I always knew someday we'd all wind up marrying and moving on, but a month ago if you had told me Mina was going to fall whole-heartedly for a guy she'd yet to meet, I'd have asked what were you smoking." Like her sister, Ginnie kept her attention on her sister and her attached-at-the-hip boyfriend.

"So when do you think he's going to pop the question?" Jo stood close enough, facing her sister so her mother wouldn't hear. Not that the whole family wasn't contemplating the same thing, their mother was just a little more intense about it. Especially at the first prospect of grandchildren. What threw Jo off balance was the sudden wide eyed look on her middle sister's face.

Pointing at the window and beyond, Ginnie blinked, snapped her mouth shut, and muttered, "Looks like now."

From where they stood in the kitchen they could see Mina standing across the yard, one hand on her chest, another over her mouth, and Kent on one knee holding a small open box in front of her. Their mother must have looked up at the same time as Ginnie. The bowl she was mixing dough in clattered into the sink as Antoinette Ummarino slapped her hands together and let out an eardrum piercing shriek. Only the huge smile that stretched from one side of her face to the other let observers know she wasn't in distress. Though she did look about ready to bust open with excitement. The woman was darting across the room and reaching for the door knob when Jo and Ginnie both lunged to grab her hand.

"At least let's wait to see what she says before we all come barreling down on them." Jo didn't dare let go of her mom's wrist.

"Of course she's going to say yes. Why wouldn't she?" Spinning in place to look out the window again, Antoinette slapped her hands together, lacing her fingers in a praying formation and lifting her gaze to the ceiling, muttered, "I'm going to be a Nonna."

"Ma!" Ginnie threw both arms up in the air and spun around, coming nose to nose with her mother. "Do not talk about babies before Mina even walks down the aisle."

"That's if she says yes," Jo added.

At that moment they all spotted Mina bobbing her head, Kent sliding the ring onto her finger as he rose to his feet.

"Grandbabies," their mom repeated.

"Mama," Jo admonished.

"Okay." Frowning, their mom flung the door open. "I won't mention babies. Yet."

On that last word she was out the door and running across the yard at full throttle.

"How long do you think she can keep the word grandbaby out of her vocabulary?"

Ginnie sighed, then chuckled softly. "I'll give her twenty-four hours."

"That long?" Jo laughed.

Like a scene in a sappy romance, Mina flung her arms around Kent as he twirled her around before setting her back on her feet and planting another one of those heart-searing kisses.

The scene had Jo sighing. Maybe her mother was right.

Maybe a man of her own and even babies wasn't such a bad idea. And maybe she should talk her sisters into another cruise. Wouldn't that be just perfect.

Enjoy an excerpt from
Heather

Heather Preston needed a good hard slap in the face—or a cold shower—or maybe both. The probability of getting enough sleep to wake up actually feeling human again made the odds *slim to none* sound favorable.

During her internship she'd come to terms with absurdly long hours. Then, as a resident, functioning on sheer adrenaline and coffee had become a way of life. Now as the attending cardiac surgeon in a major Boston hospital she'd come to accept long hours on her feet and cat naps on sofas as her forever normal—even more so since working with Doctor Michaelson, and yet today seemed bound and determined to test her limits. Not a single scheduled surgery went as expected. The valve replacement that should have only taken at most four hours had lasted well into the late afternoon. Even though she'd been thrown way off schedule, she still counted her blessings. Despite having crashed twice on the table, the patient had pulled through. Thank heaven for small miracles and the best OR team a doctor could ask for.

God willing, and as her Grams would add "if the Creek don't rise," one more person would make it home to their family. Most likely with a new appreciation for the too often overlooked precious day to day moments.

Adjusting the pager on her hip, she strolled into the break room. Waving to one of Dr. Michaelson's fellows, she tipped her head in the direction of the pot. "Fresh?"

The woman offered a friendly smile. "No, but it's strong."

"Works for me." She poured herself a cup.

"Done for the day?"

Breathing in the familiar aroma of bad coffee, Heather nodded.

"Then why aren't you on your way to the parking lot?"

"I could ask you the same thing." Lifting a shoulder in a half-hearted shrug, Heather was too tired to make the effort at hefting both shoulders and blew out a sigh. "You know how it is, simple schedule with the possibility of going home at a reasonable hour of the day and then the 10 am simple bypass turns into a quadruple backing up the day and to top it off, the 8am surgery had to be rolled back in again this evening, making a very long day even longer. All should be well, but still. I'm going to put my feet up and rest my eyelids in the on-call room, just in case we need to go back in on the 8am a third time. You, however, should go home and get some sleep. Tomorrow is an early start."

The other woman threw back the last drop of coffee and staring down at the empty cup, nodded. "Some days the coffee just isn't strong enough to keep up."

Amused by the departing words but too tired to laugh, Heather collapsed onto the well-worn sofa. She wouldn't be the first or last doctor to forego a good night's sleep in her own bed in case a patient needed her—fast. Fishing in her pocket, she pulled out her phone and debated if there was any point to going home to her own bed only to have to turn around and come back for the morning's surgery schedule.

Sliding her thumb over the glass screen, she hissed out a sigh. Not one, not two, but twelve missed calls. Almost all from her family.

The first two were from the lake house. That would be her Grandmother. The woman had a cell phone but rarely remembered to charge or carry it. A few from her sister, Violet and one from her sister Rose. A smattering from her cousins Iris and Lily. But the final missed call from the General himself, her grandfather, was the one that had her stomach pitch left then right before springing into a full-blown somersault.

"Blast." If her phone was correct, and of course there was no reason to believe it wasn't, time had gotten away from her—again. Once a month the General called and reminded her about Sunday dinner at the lake house, and every time she'd promise to do her best to make it. Growing up, having the family all home when the General was in house was the biggest deal. Attendance was not requested, it was expected. Her aunt Marissa would pack up Iris and Zinnia, swing by Boston to pick up Heather's mom with Rose, Violet and of course Heather in tow. The two sisters would grumble all the way to the lake and then spend the weekend with their sister Virginia and her four daughters, laughing and promising to stay longer next time. By the time the General retired, Sunday suppers were pretty much compulsory, but as his granddaughters had all grown up, the frequent dinners had become merely open door policy. Come if you can. The exception: the last Sunday of the month. Six days from now.

Having missed the last five months in a row, she wouldn't be surprised if the General drummed her out of the family. If only the retired military man considered saving lives a suitable excuse for failing to make an appearance, but as long as she wasn't the only surgeon on the planet, she was expected to make an appearance at least once a month.

Blowing out a long slow sigh, she closed her eyes, summoning the stamina to return the call. No nap. Her only reprieve, stalling long enough to call the land line first knowing her grandmother would be the one to answer. Since the General worshipped the ground his wife of decades walked on, reaching out to Grams before calling his cell would be the only acceptable delay that wouldn't bring censure down with a boom.

The phone rang twice before the line clicked to life.

"Hello?"

"Hi Grams, how are you?"

"Hello, dear." Two simple words and the warmth of the familiar voice soothed her tired soul. "We're hoping to see you this weekend."

"I know, but Dr. Michaelson has a fellow shadowing him this month from France and he's stacking back to back surgeries like sardines in a can."

"You do sound tired. Are you getting enough sleep? Eating right?"

The barrage of concern made Heather smile. She glanced over at the coffee pot and estimated the warm sludge she'd inhaled most likely did not constitute eating right. "I could use a nap."

"Lily's been testing new recipes for chocolate cake."

Ooh, hitting below the belt. Her cousin Lily had managed to produce the most delectable confections since her first Easy Bake Oven. Chocolate cake was Heather's weak spot and Grams knew it. She couldn't blame her grandmother for going straight for the chocolate jugular. If she had a normal nine to five job, she'd be on her way to the lake right now, but life, her life, especially now that she'd been working with the most famed cardiovascular surgeon on the Eastern seaboard, was beyond busy. There simply weren't enough hours in the day. Certainly not in days like this one. Escaping to the lake wasn't an option. Not even for Lily's latest chocolate cake creations.

In the distance a husky, male voice boomed, "Fiona?"

"I'm on the phone, dear."

"With who?"

"It's Heather, dear."

Before anyone could say another word, the General had picked up an extension and muttered her name through a momentary coughing fit.

The unexpected sound took Heather by surprise. "Are you feeling okay, General?"

"Never better," he rumbled. "We've missed you at dinner. It's been a while."

"I'm sorry. You know how things go."

"I don't." The older man tried to muffle another cough. "But I might if we ever saw you." Her grandfather's brusque tone might have concerned her more if she wasn't so fixated on why the man who never seemed to have caught even the common cold in his entire life was now trying not to hack up a lung.

"Grams, do you mind if I talk to the General for a bit?"

"Not at all. I love you, sweetie." The extension

disconnected and her grandfather coughed harder, and this time louder.

"I don't like the sound of that." Anyone else and she wouldn't have given a cough a second thought.

"It's nothing. Frog in my throat. I want to make sure you'll be here for dinner on Sunday."

She knew better than to let her grandfather deflect the conversation. "Have you been to see Dr. Wilkins?"

"That old coot? He doesn't know what ends up."

"So you've seen him?"

"I didn't say that."

"But you have. What did he say that you didn't like?" Heather asked more firmly this time. She'd learned a few things from her grandfather, and taking command over a difficult patient was easily one of them.

"Are you coming to dinner or aren't you?"

"You forgot your pills, dear," her grandmother's voice sounded in the distance.

Pills? She really didn't like the sound of this. The man didn't even believe in vitamins. Holding her breath, she quickly considered her options. Grilling the former military man on the phone would get her nowhere fast. With a little careful tap dancing, she could rearrange things at the hospital well enough to get away a few days and see what was going on for herself. Even if it was just a cold, with a man as stubborn as General Harold Hart USMC RET, pneumonia could easily become a concern if he didn't take care of himself.

"Well, young lady?" he groused.

Only her grandfather could make one of the city's most revered surgeons feel like a twelve year old caught stealing her first kiss on the family back porch. "I'll be home Sunday." *Sooner if she could make it happen.*

Warmth seeped into her grandfather's tone. "That's my girl."

Instantly, the cool deep voice of praise settled her nerves. Truth be told, she missed being home on the lake, the canopy of leaves waving hello with every breeze, the tranquil sparkle of sunlight on the water, the soothing sound of the creek trickling alongside the Point, a night of card playing or sitting on the screened-in porch with a good book and not a cell phone in sight.

Feeling better about rearranging her schedule and looking forward to a lot of chocolate cake, Heather smiled. Maybe soon she'd finally get a decent night's sleep.

Some days didn't want to cut a man a break. The brick building that housed the family hardware store was indestructible—not so much the ancient plumbing. Jake Harper had spent the better part of the morning curled into the cabinet under the bathroom sink. How he'd never noticed that in all the generations before him no one had ever installed a shut off valve was beyond him.

Now he stood balancing the new window air conditioning unit in his office in an effort to secure it before he and everything in the hundred and twenty square foot room melted under today's unseasonal spike in temperature.

"Whoa." Jake's right-hand man stepped into the blistering office. "This place is hotter than the sandbox in July."

"Tell me something I don't know."

"Got the floor in the bathroom mopped up and the shipment of blades and cutters you've been waiting for finally arrived."

"About time." Jake turned the knob to full blast and took a step back, basking in the quiet rumble and cool air blowing from the small contraption. "Much better."

"Shh," Tom chuckled. "Don't say anything or something else might break."

Earlier today, Jake had barely sat down to work on incoming inventory when the a/c unit in his office gave a sizzle and spark performance worthy of ringing in the New Year. Leaping to his feet, he'd barely unplugged the thing before it caught fire when Tom burst into the room announcing the cascading pipes. The only thing working in his favor was having the bathroom tucked far enough into a warehouse corner that the small flood hadn't had enough time to do any collateral damage to stored inventory.

The ding of the front door opening sounded and Jake spun about. "You take a well-deserved break; I'll take care of the customer."

Lawford was a small community on one of New England's best hidden lakes. There were plenty of new faces when the tourists swept in during the summer season to vacation but otherwise, Jake knew just about every local resident. Some since he was a kid working the register at his dad's side. Sadie Norton was no exception. Though until his passing about a year or so ago, it was Mr. Norton who always popped into the hardware store.

"How can I help you, Ms. Norton?"

The petite woman glanced up from the wall of hammers and offered him a shaky smile meant to show confidence. "I'm going to fix my sink."

Jake did his best to smother an amused smile. There wouldn't be much she could do to her sink with a hammer. "What seems to be the problem?"

"I'm tired of emptying the bucket under the U-tube."

It actually took Jake a second to realize she meant the P-trap. "I see."

Her gaze scanned the varying types of hammers and skimmed over to nearby saws. "I'm thinking I need one of those plumber thingies."

Okay, he might have figured out P-trap but it was more his own knowledge of plumbing than her explanation that had him guessing. "You want a pipe wrench?"

Eyes wide with confusion suddenly twinkled with satisfaction and she bobbed her head. "Yes. That's what I need."

"Have you tried calling Mike's Plumbing? I'm sure one of his guys could pop by in a minute and fix it for you."

The light in her eyes dimmed. "He's too busy for something so simple. My Bill would fix those things in a heartbeat. I'm sure I'll figure it out."

Or break something, including an arm. "You know, I'm leaving here in a few minutes, going to stop by the grocery and pick up a frozen dinner. I could stop on the way and fix that up for you in a jiffy."

"Frozen dinner? Nonsense." Her face lit up with something akin to delight. "You come straight over and while you fix the sink, I'll whip you up a good hot meal."

"If it's not too much trouble, that would be a nice change."

Straightening her shoulders, her grip tightened on her purse and her smile spread across her face. "Yes. I'm sure it will. I'd better hurry."

Jake was still watching the older woman scurry away when he almost heard Tom shaking his head.

"You do remember we have a freezer full of home cooked meals in the back."

Jake turned and smiled at his friend since kindergarten. How could he forget? There wasn't enough room in his own freezer at home for all the homemade foods he'd collected as payment over the last few months from the growing list of seniors struggling with home repairs. "What's one more sink to fix today? You don't mind closing up for me, do you?"

"Nah." Tom shook his head. Anyone who'd been deployed overseas by the Marine Corps understood the concept of a little sacrifice to help others in need. "Go fix her sink. You may want to look around for a few other things in disrepair while you're there. Her husband always seemed to be in here holding that old house of theirs together with spit, a little ingenuity, and a prayer. It may be falling down around her by now."

"That was exactly what I had in mind." He'd have to add Ms. Norton to his list. Like he told Jake, what was a little more time tucked under a sink? After a day like today there was one thing he was sure of—sleep tonight would come nice and easy.

Read more of Heather available now

MEET CHRIS

Author of over thirty contemporary novels, including the award winning Aloha Series, Chris Keniston lives in suburban Dallas with her husband and two canine children. Though she loves her puppies equally, she admits being especially attached to her German Shepherd rescue. After all, even dogs deserve a happily ever after.

More on Chris and her books can be found at www.chriskeniston.com.

Follow Chris on facebook at ChrisKenistonAuthor or on twitter @ckenistonauthor.

Join Chris' newsletter! Enjoy inside peeks and photographs from Chris' world and stories. Some times she'll thank her subscribers with a free copy of a new 99 cent flirt.

Please, if you enjoyed reading Honeymoon for Five, consider helping other readers find the Honeymoon Series by taking a moment to leave a review. Reviews are a blessing to authors and readers alike. Even just a few words will do! Thank you.